A little more of life

from within to around

Anthology Curated by

Vanshika Gupta

Inkfeathers Publishing
www.inkfeathers.com

A Little More of Life
Edited & Compiled by
Vanshika Gupta
Print Edition

First Published in India in 2022
Inkfeathers Publishing
New Delhi 110095

Copyright © Inkfeathers Publishing, 2022

ISBN 9789390882151

www.inkfeathers.com

Disclaimer

The anthology 'A Little More of Life' is a collection of 64 poems and 9 short stories written by 39 authors who belong to different parts of the world.

Unless otherwise indicated, all the names, characters, objects, businesses, places, events, incidents- whether physical/non-physical, real/unreal, tangible/ intangible in whatsoever description used in this book are either the product of the author's imagination or used in a fictitious manner. Any resemblance to actual persons, objects, entities, living or dead, or actual events is purely coincidental.

The stories and poems published in this book are solely owned by their respective authors and are in no way intended to hurt anyone's religious, political, spiritual, brand, personal or fanatic beliefs and/or faith, whatsoever. In case, any sort of plagiarism is detected in the stories and poems within this anthology or in case of any complaints or grievances or objections, neither the anthology editor nor the publisher is to be held responsible.

Contents

Part II

Part IV

Meet the Editor

A postgraduate in Economics and a writer by feels, Vanshika Gupta, also known by her pen name V, hails from the UT of Jammu and Kashmir, India. In the process of writing about anything and everything that she feels at her core, she has discovered her true self and everything else that was a blurred reality for her otherwise. She believes that words have a great power to inspire and heal and if used in the right way, they can do wonders. She mostly writes about the delicacies of a human's heart and mind and firmly believes in the idea of 'hoping against hope'. She believes in the version of a better us and the world, and with the same thought, she has created this anthology which very well depicts the idea of living and growing through this life. You can connect with her on Instagram at @v.wriiites.

Preface

A Little More of Life, as the title implies, is an anthology that is created for the purpose of spreading light and life to each and every person on this planet.

Today, we all are, in some way or the other, trapped in this world of darkness and negativity; adding to this came knocking on our doorsteps, the most devastating Coronavirus pandemic. I had never been a writer before, nor had the thought of becoming one crossed my mind in the 22 years of my existence. I did maintain my notes where I used to occasionally write down the highlights of my day, be it about the most awaited conversation or about the tight spot in my relationship with my loved ones.

I have always been a keen observer of my surroundings in general, the physical and the non-physical and the people around. If I have to be honest and truly honest, I considered myself to be the most overthinking and sentimental person in the whole, wide world and it was not just me; everyone who knew me knew this. There was a time when I used to think that being sensitive was rather an abnormality. I couldn't make peace with the fact that how people could be so indifferent. I felt everything so hard and thought that I would never be able to survive through the cruelty of human nature. Later did I realise that my sensitivity was not really my weakness, rather my utmost strength.

Thus, to be able to feel everything so deeply shouldn't be cursed, as it is the most precious gift that we have been blessed with… we just feel a little more!

The one mantra that has been getting me going through the past years is, "Feel it and free it."

Once we are aware of what it is that makes us who we are and what it is that adds on to this aspect of our personalities, it makes the answer much easier to comprehend. It was the quarantine period that had me thinking about all of it and absorbing the essence of our lives which we were just living until then, that has, today, made me a writer.

Writing about each and everything that I feel at my core – be it my relationship with people or my relationship within; be it my take on things and topics sensitive to society; be it humanity and practicality or be it nature and everything related to it – the process has made me discover my true self along with everything else that was a blur reality for me, otherwise.

I absolutely believe in this idea of 'vibing with life'. Given the making of this anthology, I chose this theme because I truly want the world to believe that no matter how bad things are today, if we choose to look on the brighter side and try to vibe with this life, it will never disappoint us.

You may have gone through literal heartbreaks or loss of near and dear ones, or anxiety, or peer pressure, or self-made obligations, or societal pressure, or destructive criticism, and what not! Then, how do you get along with life? What is that secret ingredient that gives you your strength and will? It will vary from person to person because the process of healing is not really a code to ensure by. For me, I found my solace in writing my heart out. So, not making healing the hype-word, how would you describe your healing process? Because remember, healing won't take your sparkle away, rather it will make you shine admirably.

When we talk about it, isn't the idea of 'A Little More of Life' too diverse and quite empathetic at the same time?

Bringing to you 'A Little More of Life' is an attempt of 39 wonderful writers to tell their tales of self-discovery and never-ending hope. Divided into 4 parts, each part contains a collection of poems, articles, and stories that are like songs of the respective writers' faith and hope in humanity and the universe, moreover in themselves, and these will help the readers to find their answers of living and learning through their lives.

How nice would it have been if we could be the perfect hosts to our own imperfectly perfect selves?

If we could be completely honest with our insecurities or maybe if we were courageous enough to open our hearts again!

What or where would be the perfect abode for us?

Because it's you who you have been looking for, your perfect home!

May you all find it soon.

Happy journey!

Part I

~ Evolving with the obscure,

Defying the established norms,

Following the changing course ~

The Path to Self-Discovery

by Arijit Dey

The process of finding the real you or self-discovery is a topic less talked about in this day and age. The first thing that pops up in my mind is whether I can find it in school or any other prestigious educational institute, because we are accustomed to this pattern of learning, and stopping after we are done with that course of action. But let me tell you that neither school nor any other esteemed institution would help us with that search; it is something which never really existed in the curriculum. Not even would it be your parents or any beloved one. *It must be you who will find the 'real you', treading the untrodden path.*

The ones who have achieved that stage have led to a home run in life. And what a generation to be born around, surrounded by successful entrepreneurs and such eminent personalities who believed in themselves and found their true selves, acted upon it, and made it big! It need not be something as big as a business idea, it can even be our character or our disposition for which we can be proud of; that small ray of hope that gathers us and never lets us fall apart, even after going through several setbacks in our lives.

We are born in a society which is led by rules and stereotypes. Everything is pre-defined in a manner, as if we all are enacting some kind of role in this so-called 'drama of life'. As Mahatma Gandhi once rightly said, "We but mirror the world. All the tendencies present in the outer world are to be found in the world of our body. If we could change ourselves, the tendencies in the world would also change." Similarly, we can't change the system, but we can bring the change within ourselves.

Since the world we are living in is too complex to be cognizant of, the moment we try to go beyond, we promptly become vulnerable to the unwanted opinions, guidance, and judgement. But a little more of hope and faith in ourselves can lead us the way. We often underestimate ourselves and the potential with which we are born.

Everyone is special in their own unique way. You may be a mosaic piece who is trying to fit in, but if you have ever visited any architectural place, you must have observed that even those messed up fittings can do wonders and tell you a beautiful story. Some build careers to search for their true selves, throwing themselves into critical situations and gaining experiences out of it, while some put their feelings on paper as if they were the 'next Shakespeare', hoping for people to read and acknowledge, while some move towards spiritual awakening. But all in all, everyone is doing something or the other in this journey of self-discovery.

If you still haven't thought about it, the first thing you need to do is START.

Start with what you love doing. Start within your comfort zone and then gradually transcend your habitat, you'll surely reach your destination. Interact with people, share ideas, grab some of them, and implement whatever suits you the best.

In this process, you may need to learn, unlearn, and relearn over and over, so be ready for that. At times, you may get trapped in that vicious cycle of self-doubt and dejection where you may not get the results as and when expected and everything seems to be an attempt in vain; but that is completely fine.

At one point, every single person feels the void in some sort or the other. Try quitting your present work and opt for something completely different. (In short, take a break.)

You just need to pick up the colours of your choice and start painting the blank canvas with something that cheers your soul up. I do agree that some folks are born with in-house talent, but others explore through their journey of life and then find their answers in the pathway.

Just trust the process.

Life is the ocean; you are the diver and self-discovery is the pearl underneath. I know it's easy to just state this but trust me when I say, "Why become like someone else when you can be the next you?'

BE THE NEXT YOU!

A Perspective

by Rinku Tyagi

Stemming from my subconscious
A thought roots itself deep
Impregnates a seed of doubt
In my mind while asleep.

My vision, my beliefs
And all that I care
Are they really insane?
Or an insanely real nightmare?

Observing the horizon, I see
Breezy dawn, alluring sunset
The magnitude of events
Leaves me puzzled and upset.

Paying attention to detail
What others feel, I wonder
What is existential for me, I guess
Do I even exist, they even ponder?

A spec in the canvas
A grain in the sand
My place in this gargantuan world
Is something I fail to understand.

I wonder how my nose looks
I think it's pointy and straight
When others plainly descry
They don't find it so great.

Hearing my euphonious voice
My heart swells with pride
I stop because I'm asked to
Leaves me flushed, wanting to hide.

A peek in the mirror slyly reveals
Things I conjure and foolishly desire
A squinty eye and skin that peels
All I find behind that exquisite attire.

Exceptional and prodigious
My world as I pretend
Insipid and dreary, for others
It is to no end.

A Quest for Silence

by Rinku Tyagi

Silence matters
Silence shatters
Louder than words
The echo that clatters.

The world so deafening
Peace and calm are gone
Quiet and tranquil
Not even when I'm alone.

People clamouring
Buildings rattling
Shrieking in the ears
Even the whispers piercing.

Banging against the walls
The prisoner of my mind
Resonating in the emptiness
My inner self stuck in the grind.

Body struggles
Mind boggles
To sync the two
My spirit often buckles.

Fleeing from the commotion
Weary soul wants relief
No rest, no escape
Endless agony, my belief.

Turbulence in me
Turbulence outside
Quietude can be gained
By lulling the heartache inside.

Dawn Arising

by Kruttika R. Hegde

Backpacking
Through fields, absurdly yellow
Burnt under the summer sun
Running with an urgency
To some destination
Beyond comprehension
Tall grass and distant hills
The land rolls up and down while I run
Sun is setting on time
And a new one about to rise
But darkness must come between
Shrouding the distant rolling hills
Stars begin to haunt the sky
Ghostly pale the moon I see, arise
Backpacking through miles
Of open land

I'm running, far and wide
A quest of my own
A secret land from dreams
I'm chasing wild into the unknown
Running through an open land
Running into a dawn arising.

Dreamer

by Ashon Calhoun

For what it's worth, we're too quick to seal our dreams in the dirt
We say the sky's the limit, yet we bury the sky in the earth
Come to terms, I know that reality burns
Waiting to be great and then reality turns
The death of a dream that is what reality mourns
Despite mourning, in the morning, I know I'll believe my dreams again
No hocus pocus, no losing focus, only tunnel vision to the end
Whispers in my ear, killing a dream, I don't know what's expected
They kill a dream, and it's dead until I decide it's resurrected
I hope I don't choke, and my dreams are not affected
But if I do lose hope, I'll know it was by reasons that I suspected
Hard to believe, I've got dreams that are hard to achieve
Success does not come by rest, so it's hard to succeed
But I'm a dreamer!

Ella's Courage

by Nuzhat Reza

Can I not just say out loud?

With no fear of judgement or conviction.

Day in and day out, I look at myself in the mirror.

Hey, you missy! I say, you are perfect and fair!

But they are all lies, my baby girl.

You have now become a woman in a domain that is a terror.

Heart of gold you have, and a mind full of dreams and wit.

But courage is what's buried, in a gold mine which is dark and
deep.

No! You say, you shout and scream.

No! You say, as gentle as one could be.

Your heart is as light as a feather, and warm as the rays of the sun.

But when the tempest befalls, the fire of Phoenix ignites and lights
up your courage, hidden so deep and strong.

Yes, you are strong my baby girl, more than you know.

Be the love you carry in your heart and the breath of fresh air in
the autumn spring.

Be the first light of dawn and the sunset at the sea.

Be the star you were born to be, the crying shoulder when
someone in need.

Be the happiness you are, the courageous, dreamer and the queen
you are meant to be.

Expectations

by Rinku Tyagi

Expectation crumples personality
Futile as a used napkin
Flung carelessly, not to be
Comprehended or regarded
Under any circumstance whatsoever.
Expectations, yours, piled up
With those of others
Warp your character
Bludgeoning it with hammer
Of self-doubt and worry.

The dark clouds of suspicion
Wall the straggling boughs
Of your personality
Fence the prisoner from blooming
Into the hues of singularity
Obscure the fortifying radiance
Of the soothing sun
That pushes the fragile roots of your character
To the depth of sublimity.

Victim of such predicament
Forlorn spirits in vermillion bars
Forever swirling in the maelstrom
Of predilections and anticipation
Scaling the towering stack
Of staggeringly high hopes.

Hollow hopes prance around, since
The bashful soul sets her trembling feet
On the much demanding threshold
Of the newly vowed life.
Struggling hard, reeling from
The tireless dilemma
Filling the unfathomable belly
Of the voracious evil.
Life turns complacent
Blind to the lightning magnification
The world sprung into
Outside her marital circumference.

Desires turn into embers, searing
Constantly in the domestic furnace
Wants and needs abandon the abode
Weary of the unabated neglect.
Happiness succumbs
To the innumerable lacerations
To pride and dignity, clambering the
Unsurmountable peak of expectations.

And still, the hideous Medusa devil
Refuses to die or subside
Continues to feed on incessant sacrifices
On the altar of holy matrimony.

Her Steely Eyes

by Kruttika R. Hegde

There she was, her hair blew
Wild about her face
Steely eyes looked at the world
That did her harm.
Warm was her heart, still refusing to see the dark
Golden her soul for she loved yet
Despite all that was meted out to her.
Steps so sure, she wanted only
To spread the light
Love she had only
For she had learnt its power.
Her steely eyes looked at the world
Light spread from where she stood.

Human

by Rinku Tyagi

I met a little girl
Presently, if at all
Just in a reverie
Or a thought, as I recall.

A chill runs down my bone
Makes me sweat and shiver
Strange, familiar she seems
Who was she? I ponder.

Myself, my own self
Naive and plain
Unrefined, true to her spirit
Free from all constraints.

Still gathering, still curious
Always learning, always furious
Couldn't fathom, couldn't contain
Wouldn't stop, wouldn't restrain.

Never mild, always bitter
Doesn't mince her words ever
Straight and honest to a fault
Reckless and carefree, by default.

Rising from the dream
My reality strongly strikes
Toughened facade conceals
Feeble heart, no one likes.

Tempered with grief
Softened by pain
Lulled by pensiveness
Poignant disposition, I gain.

Sanguine attitude soars high
Moral rectitude runs deep
Adamant endeavour towards perfection
Assumed precedence, takes a leap.

A cloak of happiness, I embrace
A mask of smile, I wear
Put on a disguise of perfection
To conceal all frailties unclear.

All errors and flaws endless
And a dash of goodness combined
Mixed in unbalanced proportion
Makes me a human, in body and mind.

I Wish

by Rinku Tyagi

Home alone, I discern
I have many wishes
Yet to be fulfilled
Ironical it is, limited are the means
For stuck in a bubble
Life as it seems.

Explicitly, I sense
Rise in the need
To explore the limits
Of my vagrant self
Not much I care
To explicate the intensity
Which fibrillates my very identity.

If I could permeate
Through the rigidity
Of the bony cage
And transcend
Through the realms
Of my dreamy escapades
I would achieve
The sublimity I craved.

In Hindsight

by Vanshika Gupta

Sliding over the busy route
Slipping into nothingness
A trembling sensation rushes through my veins
Taking me back to the Ferris wheel
Somewhere far away, and yet too close.

How quiet is this place!
That I can feel all the numbness at its best
The whirring of fireflies echoing in my heart
The silent screams in my head
Making their presence more eminent.

Where do I belong?
Not able to make it out
Confronting the demons in and out
Clinging onto the beliefs
Thinking of ways to complete this round.

Fighting against the dark
I finally find the light
Digging into my soul
Where faith is restored
In hindsight
I attain my lost sight.

Dissolving into the fire
Merging with the unruffled nature
Caressing life
Through the meadows and the gravels
I get in.

In Pursuit of Happiness

by Zoya Hussain

Trying to map the territories
Of an unknown, far-fetched land,
I wandered places
The mundane life
The banal schedule
The trickery of the subconscious
Made me wander all the more
The more I wandered
The less I knew
They asked me a zillion questions
All in vain.

All the more and all the less
Until one day, whence came a reflection
Made me free off the shackles
Of all my doubts
In retrospect,
When I saw it everywhere
Almost everywhere

Through latent
The eyes that could seed it
The mind that could live it
The heart that could feel it.
In the monk's sermon
In the dead silence of the valley
In the sound of the deep's crickets
In Neruda's quietness and Plath's Mirrors
In Dante's comedy and Bard's tragedy
The hanging ivy
The still wind chimes
The poor child, the wailing mother
The cemetery, the maternity
That dim star, the moving galaxy
Everywhere
Yes, they were mine
The eyes, heart, and mind
That had it
What?
The same nine letter emotion
I was in pursuit of.

Perils of An Introvert

by Yesha Dave

As humans, we have a propensity towards comparing our lives with others. Quite so often, we let anyone's opinion affect our confidence and the narrative of who we are. Sofia Gallagher—an American teenager whose creativity was crumpled by society—struggled throughout her childhood with accepting herself.

Right from dressing up the way others did to losing her individuality to conform—she completely lost track of herself and her originality. Sofia never let anyone know about her plight; yet, people were ruthless, and bullied her. She was an under-average performer academically; however, she had a mind full of imagination succumbed by judgment. Growing up, it was not at all easy for her to gain self-confidence.

"I am just sick of all the past experiences that are haunting me right now!" Sofia initiated the conversation after sitting in her therapist's room for 5 minutes. "It's not as easy as it sounds; I am almost 20 with low self-esteem and no faith in myself. All I want is for people to be kind and think once before talking crap!" she sobbed.

Her therapist, Mrs. Shawn, had been treating Sofia since she was 16. Sofia's mother signed her up for therapy after a terrifying episode that happened in her middle school.

Sofia was bullied throughout her childhood and middle school. The famous girls, like we all watch in movies, made living hell for Sofia. They would embarrass her in front of boys, laugh at her academic performance, and hurl insults for being an introvert. It was traumatic for an emotional and sensitive person like Sofia. One fine day, things got out of hand when one of the girls—a rich, spoiled brat—deceived her into wearing an uncomfortable outfit for the annual play. There were professors, parents and fellow peers who felt that things had got too far. This left a deep scar in Sofia's mind, heart, and soul.

"Sofia, you do not need anybody's validation. You are strong enough to break through the idea of people disliking you. Maybe they are just jealous of you and worry that if they don't suppress your talent, you may outperform them. Give this a thought." Mrs. Shawn consoled her.

Sofia met with her twice a week for an hour which most of the time would go up to 2 hours. Initially, she had a hard time finding the right words, but with time, she was able to express herself in a better way. Mrs. Shawn would make her journal her thoughts or record herself whenever she felt agitated.

"In your previous video, you broke down because you felt ugly and didn't see any hope. Let this sink in: there is no such thing as ugly! The mindset of people is ugly, the way they perceive the world is ugly, the way they treat other people is ugly. You need to stop browsing through social media—it is fake. You don't know the people you are seeing on social media. What's their reality? Do you have any idea? So, let go of this comparison and competition and see the change in your life," Mrs. Shawn asserted.

Sofia's rendezvous with her therapist certainly changed her, in that she started loving herself more often. Indeed, there were days when she didn't feel good about herself, but on most days, she started being gentle on herself. This is what life is all about—be the change you want to bring! Sofia wanted people to treat her with kindness, but she had aways been hard on herself. Once she embraced her reality and changed her perception, she became confident enough to let go of all that was not serving her well and eventually found everything that she was looking for in the wrong places, in herself.

Into the Random Mess

by Vanshika Gupta

Vanishing into the random mess
Trying to interpret the rhythm
Debating over my identity
In order to understand the procedure
The light, the dark
The shadow, the spark
Forming a new melody of the drizzling fears
Failing attempts to make it better
Amidst the hide and seek of the truth
Disguising the reality with mere facts
Wishing nothing but brightness ahead
Without following the crucial process
Continuous downpour from the sky
Causing my flight, a doomed rise
Hoping for a smooth course of existence

Beyond the subject of matter and life
An endeavour to evolve into my highest self
Failing to remember the purpose
Vanishing into the random mess
Trying to interpret the rhythm
Debating over my identity
In order to fathom the discrepancy
Of the known and the unknown.

Ironclad Smiles

by Aditi Rao

I was mould from an egg to a beautiful bird
Free to fly and free to surge
I waited my time in your womb, Mama
No one, oh, no one, could have my happiness purged.

They told me I was broken and slightly deformed
Three instead of two, the tubes had formed
They messed up my functions and caused me pain
I laughed at their faces that showed horror in vain.

I'm a bird, you fools! I smiled on
Happy, adorable, fearless, and strong
I was given a life to spread joy and love
I'm not deformed, I'm a special dove.

I was chosen for this test, though it's hard to believe
I'm stronger, I'm bolder, and I've passed the sieve
Put your worries to rest, I'm healthy, I breathe
I'll smile through it all, till the troubles seethe.

Life is bigger than these temporary trials,
Why are you afraid? Of the needles and the vials?
He knew we were fighters of the Pandey Clan
We smile, we laugh, no filters, no scans.

I'm a miracle you fools, I'll not be let down
I was born with more courage than tubes can drown
I'll pass, I'll fly, and I'll challenge the frowns
I'm not afraid of the smell, the needles, and the gowns.

Don't you worry, Mama, I'm yours to keep
Lay your heart to rest, you smile, you sleep
It's a new day tomorrow, I'll beat the odds
They will all be clapping, while you laugh through the nods.

Life: A Wish To Live For

by Apurav Mahajan

I wish I could be wise,
For myself to be precise.
And if I had a choice,
To decide for my own life.

My heart aches for a win,
A win just to begin.
But to my chagrin,
I was nowhere to be seen.

My mind screams for peace,
Maybe only on a lease.
Only wish I could release,
All of my caprice.

I wish I could be wise,
As my heart and mind surmised.
I wish I dismissed the strife,
To decide for my own life.

Like A Lotus

by Vanshika Gupta

Giving up every now and then
Rushing towards my favourite, dark deserted den
Unable to decipher if it is the reality or my escape
Making me forlorn in almost every case
A rollercoaster of possibilities guiding my lane
The dilemma of choosing now goes in vain
Figuring out the essence of my survival in main

After all, what is life without its certain highs and lows?
I prefer to bloom like a lotus with glow
Making growth the mantra of this life's ebb and flow.

Mask-Off

by Vanshika Gupta

The one thing that I want to feel but I shouldn't
Drags me into this abyss of endless pros and cons
I wish I could tear apart this fallacy
That leads me to rot
Sloughing off the masquerade
To contort my individuality once again.
Brutal but honest
Exploiting the naked truth
Yet again, fuelling this disdain
To simplify the reasons of my existence
In the most subtle way.

For I exist with faults and flaws
I should have unravelled their cause
For I am still surviving
To watch this mask fall off
With all the rush that surrounds my soul
So fine, so pure.
To witness with my eyes wide closed

That I still have a long way to go
To rule out the possibility
Of not being aware
That it was neither threatening, nor liberating
To protect myself from the masked devil
Who often makes me a stranger in my own sight
So, I am learning to live more by the sunrise
To swamp my heart with its warmth so divine
Making me believe that the bad nights will pass
And I will rise again to paint my odyssey
Quelling the midnight crisis.

Out of Place, Out of Mind

by Vanshika Gupta

Never thought that it would feel so out of place
When the only thing that kept me sane
Became the reason today
Why I am so insane
It was easy to believe in its grace
Until the reality unveiled its true face
Blaming the fate was not so sincere
When the mind was already lost in a fair
Stressing out was no more a job
Because there was more chaos in the mob
Something was there that did not fit that phase
When all the clues were left in the maze
Never thought that the heart would close its gate
Only when I wondered if I was too late
To wake up from my dream
Just so I could not sabotage my esteem
Not anymore.

She

by Simran Gupta

A little girl with her own ways to be happy never knew what life
had for her
All her mind could think was about her favourite food
And that was all she preferred.

Then she grew a little by age and a little more by weight
But for her, the weight gain didn't matter
All that mattered was the doubt if her weight could affect her fate.

Well by this time, she grew all fat and the people, the society made
her feel as if it was a sin
With the desolation and dejection, all she could hope for was
getting her favourite gin.

She no longer found her body beautiful
For beautiful had its own definition in their minds
Frustrated and hopeless, she blamed herself for being the way she
was.

With passing time, everything changed except one thing,
The humiliation from the folks, from her own people and pals.

Of course, this couldn't last for long
There had to be a breakdown and this feeling had to end
The day of self-acceptance finally came where she stopped herself
to defend.

She knew no matter what happens, people will always judge
If not weight, then by colour or height and what not!

Now, her fight was over with the people, the society
And the journey to an end of body shaming meant a lot.

Don't you think it was high time to come out in the world all by
herself
And put an end to all the cribbing and vulnerability?
The question was no longer to the world, but to herself and no one
else.

So, here it is, the 'she' I am referring to is not some other girl but
me
And you have no idea, letting this out makes my spirit free.

I know people will eventually forget my pain
My struggle to live each day and my side of the story.

But guess what,
Now none of it really matters because
A bunch of heartless people cannot affect my glory.

This is Me Trying

by Vanshika Gupta

Fading with a gentle breeze
My feet freezing in turmoil
This is me trying
To let this rustling sound
Take all my reasons away.

Tick tock tick tock
Rushing through a flood of emotions
This is me trying
To forget your echoes
Chiming in my mind.

Dissipating with the shimmering sand
Standing here with my bare hands
This is me trying
To free myself
From this woven cage of insecurities.

Hoping to catch your rays
Wishing to breathe in your grace
This is me trying
To embrace your warmth
Even though you are nowhere close.

Admiring the butterflies dancing in the sky
Forgetting about all its highs
This is me trying
To paint my life
With all the bright shades
Without missing any of its greys.

Through the Winter Night

by Matali Mahajan

A gusty wind hit my hind
Froze my spine
With all its might
As I walked through the winter night.

Whispering in my ears
About the upcoming dares
"I shall overcome them,"
Said my eyes' glare
Soaked in fear
With misty tears
"I will not give up,"
Said my trembling valour
As I walked through the winter night.

Trying to survive that stormy sight
I learnt to depend on my own shoulders
With nothing but pride
Watching the moon so bright

The darkness behind enhanced its shine
While the wintry wind mesmerized my mind
As I walked through the winter night.

The will like a raincoat
Rose from my inside
Shielding the anxiety
Drizzling in my mind
As I walked through the winter night.

New day came with the clouds so clear
"You won we lost,"
They whispered in my ear
As I walked past that winter night
I flew so high
Like a bird in white
Through the mist
I fought it right.

Unfettered

by Tashu Malik

Want to put miles between myself
And the other me
Who wants to run free
Unfettered
Chasing breezes
Which rustle the soul
Sitting beneath dewdrops
Waiting for them to fall
From the morning leaves
Onto my half-asleep dreams
Floating with the frolicking streams
Before they go on to be rivers so deep
Resting in the green of trees old
Who have stories plenty, untold
Of those who have run through the space
Unfettered and free

Of moments that existed only to exist
Without leaving traces of history
Beyond those miles
Will I find that other me?
Living unfettered, unbound, and free.

Yes! I Found Me

by Pratheepa Kannan

Life was a straight line
With guidance it went fine.
Never thought to appeal
Only was taught to seal.
Etched in heart as a rule
Tied up was the soul.
As days went,
The knot at the throat tightened.
Always threw a smile
Hiding the suffocation inside.
On a day everything I built
Went crashing down.
I threw away the blindfold
Forced by society.
Finally opening the shutter
To the flooding inquisitiveness
Of my puerile mind to the world.
The emotions which evolved around the
Established norms widened

Through the crevices of global knowledge.
Why settle for the good?
When I deserve the best
The heart inside
Chuckled with confidence.
Here I come! The world
With the flattering
Noise of the inner me.
I razed every hurdle that
Meddled with my revision.
None deserve to be contained!
None deserve to be overpowered!
None deserve to be judged!
It is not the world, but me!
Who destroyed my inner power.
The hesitation, fear, and inferiority complex
Withheld my own ability.
Who am I to blame?
If the societal rule is crippled
I am to use my own limbs.
The day I let go of the hold
I relied on,
Is the day I really lived.

Empurpled

by Dani Hudson

Purple has been the color to dominate my existence. Pre-determinism is what I would call it. By the time I was ready to make the journey from my mother's womb, my grandmother sewed a lavender blanket that was bordered with a lace trim and embroidered with Mother Goose in the centre. Twenty-five years later, I still fall asleep with that blanket balled up in my arms every night.

My mother's favorite color was purple, that's probably why I initially took a liking to it. It was the first color I was able to distinguish from the others. Purple is the color of the crown chakra and now that my mom is gone, my only way to reach her is through these psychic cords that manifest in a purple hue. However, recently, I learned that the seven-chakra system was curated by some white guy to make a system more digestible for the Western world, so maybe it's all bullshit, anyway. Either way, sometimes I just want something to believe in.

That blanket was with me as I cried at my first three sleepovers at the neighbor girl's house when I was seven; a few bodies of boys I brought back to my college dorm when my roommate was away; the boys I broke up with so I could continue living the fast life; a few girls too; it saw the figures that lurked in the night as I lay paralyzed in fear; the nights I came back to bed blackout drunk and forgot to position it in the way I like the most.

I can remember a specific day in the first grade. My teacher scheduled "pilgrim day" around the Thanksgiving holiday, in which every kid brought a blanket from home to sit on the floor and dress in costumes. All the students sat in a circle on the floor on our own blankets and I, of course, with my special purple one. One of our activities was to churn butter as a class. The teacher piled in all the dairy fat she could into a single mason jar then dropped a marble inside before placing the lid on top. She shook the jar for about 30 seconds in her dainty, pale hands and then passed it onto the student sitting eagerly beside her. Every student got a turn to shake the jar to help with the churning process. By the time the jar got to me, I was quaking with excited nervous energy. All eyes on me as I took the centre stage in the churn circle. I shook and I shook the jar until the glass could no longer withstand the rattling of the 6-year-old hands and all the milky contents spilled over my lap and my purple blanket. After a moment of shock, this event unraveled my emotions. The horror and embarrassment sent my little self drowning in tears, and my teacher took me to the bathroom to clean off and calm me down.

I miss the days when I was allowed to be expressive of my emotional state. Kids are granted the privilege of emotional outbursts at things that are new or out of the ordinary. But that's not the case for adults. If my eyes were to well up in front of my peers because I couldn't open the jar of cherry jam that I was committed to at the moment when I finally decided to eat my first meal of the day, then people would see me as unstable; when really, it's the small things that send reverberations of the greater losses we face. But since I live here and now, my emotional state has become a performance for others.

I write about purple not because it necessarily brings me comfort, but simply because it always seems to be around. Recently, hyper consumerism grabbed me by the throat and suffocated me until I bought an iPhone to make myself feel better about my recent shortcomings. Though it looks like every other phone on the planet, it at least has a cute, soft purple backing to it. This phone is within my eyesight 24x7. It's never not on me and truthfully, I can feel my cortisol levels rise if I am separated from it at any point in time. It's my sole connection to the world and I would give my life for it. This electronic purple brick is an extension of my being.

I would humbly state that some of the greatest songs ever made were entitled with the word "purple." Jimi Hendrix had 'Purple Haze', Portugal the Man had 'Purple Yellow Red and Blue'; Gogol Bordello had 'Start Wearing Purple'. Prince's 'Purple Rain' was the last song he performed two weeks before he passed away. I, and I'm sure many others, always associated Prince with the color purple. I once read that the Byzantines would use the phrase "born into the purple" when describing those born into the upper echelons of society. An ounce of purple was once worth its weight in gold since it was so meticulous to produce and hard to come by. Only royalty could afford to spend their dimes on the mysterious hues excreted by miniscule sea snails. Not hard to see why an artist who wants to be known as "Prince" would capitalize on purple to build their character.

I find Purple Rain to be one of the few power ballads I can really enjoy, a song that I find myself being completely lost inside of. In the second half of the song, the band riffs for about 3 minutes straight; in the last minute, Prince comes back in to add some prolonged "hoo hoos" to add a new layer to the music and complete the sound. I find this to be the most entrancing part of the song. His voice is the perfect accent for this piece, evoking emotion that no words could. As Ludwig Wittgenstein once wrote, "If only you do not try to utter what is unutterable, then nothing gets lost. But the unutterable will be unutterably contained in what has been uttered." So, whatever it is that Prince was trying to say to us in that piece of music, he did so perfectly without saying a word.

In college, I began my curiosities in healing stones. Amethyst was the first stone I invested in. I can remember walking into some Pagan bookstore and my eyes being drawn to that stone amongst the others. When I held it in my hand, I expected to feel a surge of energy flowing between me and it. But all I could feel were the jagged edges of the stone. I bought a small one for about three dollars. Maybe I just needed to take it home so we could get to know each other more. We found one another at a time in life where I needed protection from the world. I had fallen victim to a series of bad luck events, and I needed something to bring myself back up. Amethyst is said to activate spiritual awareness, enhancing intuition and psychic abilities. To no surprise, it's linked to the crown chakra, but my mom was still around then. At that time, I wondered if a spiritual quest, starting with a purple stone, would help me to have faith in myself once again.

Part II

~ Someone to cherish endlessly,
To live it all for courageously,
And call it your home religiously ~

A Monochromatic Fanatic

by Raghav Mahajan

Okay! I confess, I am slightly obsessed

I am a monochromatic fanatic

Of the green, grey hues

I get lost in your shades

I can stare at them for days

For weeks, months and the rest of my years

They are beautiful, even with tears

But my heart skips a beat

When they sparkle with laughter

My soul fills with pearls

When I look inside to see the little girl

You try so hard to hide

She is not hidden; she lives in your eyes

And I know, I can spend the rest of my life

Drowning in the deep colourful pools

Of your precious jewels

They beautifully mirror mine

And will forever be my only lifeline.

Chasm of the Cryptic

by #Ra

Sitting alone in his happy dome
His thoughts were cryptic
Because she was mystic!
He dived deep and deep into the thoughts
Leaving behind all the odds
All the sparks ignited were so fine
Like vibrant wind chimes
The funny thing they shared was a timeline.

She was a temple of thoughts
And made him learn to embrace and defy the odds
Analytic, Catalytic, Altruistic – a silent fireball she was
On a whole novelistic baa.

But the fate was decided
Sparks didn't reside
Moving to and fro
Slowly got faded in a row
Heartbreak, sorrow and what not

All formed a canopy of sad thoughts
But these didn't let him down in any kind
As he still carries her beautiful thoughts in his mind
His fondness was infinite and blind
So, he built a fort for her in the universe of his mind
Where she blissfully lives in a fine chime.

Now embracing the thoughts, he only had
Enjoying every bit of life, even loving the bad
All this came like bustling fireflies
Because her thoughts enchanted, "A Little More of Life"!

His thoughts had to be cryptic
Because she was mystic!

Eclipse

by Rohan P. Lapalikar

When the light around you is gone
And the darkness doesn't let you see
Even then, I will find you
And be your torch and set your fears free.

When the strength in you is gone
And the demons don't let you sleep
Even then, I will find you
And be your happiest dream that you can keep.

When the paths you take
Lead to nowhere and you feel adrift
Even then, I will find you
And be the ray of light for you to uplift.

When the dark clouds show
And eclipse your presence
Even then, I will find you
And tell the Sun about your existence.

When the time is hard
And efforts go in vain
Even then, I will find you
And give you every ounce of faith I have gained.

When your colours will fade
And crayons are no longer of use
Even then, I will find you
And be the rainbow of hues.

When people will abandon
And the world turns its back on you
Even then, my love, I will find you
And be the home that will protect you.

Because trust me, my love,
Even if our hands are tied in a rope
Our destiny cannot deny the fact
That you are my only hope.

I'll Take You to A Morning Walk

by Vishal Nagpal

I'll take you to a morning walk.
Don't you snooze that alarming clock!
Night surrendering; darkness withdrawn!
I know, you'll yawn,
Did you imagine the mesmerising, tinted dawn?

I'll take you to a morning walk.
You'll hop over the sideway chalk.
It will be fun.
You'll see the sun.
The sun and its warm shine.
The cold breeze will refill life in your spine.

I'll take you to a morning walk.
A brisk walk to your favourite park.
I'll tell that dog not to bark.
Don't you love the birds' talk!

I'll take you to a morning walk.
A brisk walk to your favourite park.
Where there are heaps of the fallen leaves.
Each leaf on the ground that never grieves.

I'll take you to a morning walk.
A brisk walk to your favourite park.
Don't you want to see that colourful flower?
Which tells you every hour,
that your true colour is your own power!

"I'll take you to a morning walk!"
It's a note to myself,
– A 'me-to-me' talk!

Self-Love is Not Selfish

by Namrata Agarwal

I have always lived a busy life. From working in an MNC to starting my brand, I never had time for myself. Since I launched my brand in May 2018, I never took a week off and worked all days. The only break I ever took was when I had to attend weddings. It was mentally exhausting, and then hit Covid-19. I was staying away from my family, and my business had paused. For the first time in my life, I had nothing to do. Being locked up in my apartment for so many months with literally no human contact, I started feeling lonely. Hence, I started reading articles on self-help and watched videos of motivational speaker Jay Shetty. His famous book 'Think Like a Monk' was released around that time. I ordered it off Amazon and started reading it. I listened to his podcast 'On Purpose with Jay Shetty'. It opened a whole new world for me. I felt like there was so much in the world I knew nothing about. I was so glad that I found him. I learned a lot of things from his book and podcast.

Before I get into that, let me share how they helped me. I became calmer, happier, and relaxed throughout the day and slept better through the night. I became more patient. I started to pause and respond instead of reacting. I stopped giving attention to trivial matters. I started directing my energy towards things and people who mattered while becoming a lot more productive.

Here are a few things I learnt and try to follow regularly:

Self-Love

I have always been a believer in self-love. Reading these books and articles made me feel how important it is to always love ourselves. We judge ourselves way too much – our weight, how we look, our complexion, our job and what-not. We punish ourselves. We forgive others even though we never forgive our own selves. It is time we cut ourselves some slack and accept ourselves for who we are. We look for love from others and give unconditional love to others. We must learn to love ourselves the same way. We need to know so much about ourselves before letting anyone in our lives. Self-love is not selfish. We must take ourselves to the movies, for shopping, for dinner. It is okay to do grand gestures for ourselves the way we do it for others. It is okay for us to gift flowers to ourselves or bake a cake or have an ice cream by ourselves. We deserve it.

Meditation

While many may find it difficult to concentrate, meditation helps calm our minds. Just focusing on our breathing as we inhale and exhale helps our body, reduces anxiety and stress. It is acceptable if we get consumed by our thoughts while we meditate or get distracted by sounds around us or if we open our eyes. There is no perfect way of doing meditation. There is no judgment if we cannot focus as long as we are willing to try.

Here is how I practice it every day:

I put on some nice and relaxing music. I light scented incense sticks (my personal favourite is Patchouli fragrance), open my windows so natural light can come in. I find a comfortable place to sit, straighten my back and loosen all my muscles. I close my eyes and focus on breathing & then I inhale for a count of 4 and exhale for a count of 4. As I try to meditate, I think of different scenarios. For example, I try to visualize the room I am sitting in, sitting in front of the mountains, walking on a beach. I think of fond memories and try to recreate them in my mind as I meditate. The possibilities are endless. I usually meditate for about 15–20 minutes. As I am done, I rub my palms to make them warm and place them on both my eyelids before I open my eyes. The best time to meditate would be mornings because it gives a great start to the day. It keeps us calm, positive, and centred throughout the day. We feel more energetic and can work better.

Gratitude

Gratitude is the ultimate key to happiness. Being thankful for what we have rather than what we lost puts things into perspective. We can feel grateful for our body for so much that it does for us, for having a roof over our heads, for having food on our tables. We can be thankful for the sun, the moon, and the stars. It is tough to feel grateful when we are going through a bad day. Hence, I strongly recommend maintaining a Gratitude Journal to write down all the great things we have in our lives. On tough days, we can flip through those pages. It helps change our mood and find motivation.

Here is how I practice it every day:

After my morning meditation, I thank God for giving me yet another day to live and for other things that I feel grateful for at that moment. Before I go to bed, I write down three things that I am thankful for, anything good that happened on that day. Morning gratitude helps in having a great start to the day and night-time gratitude helps with better sleep.

Affirmations

Affirmations are a great way to motivate ourselves. It means saying positive statements such as - I am strong. I am healthy. I love myself and likewise. Saying positive affirmations help put us in a positive state of mind. It gives us a nice boost. It is said that life is what happens for us and not to us. Hence, we must always surround ourselves with positive thoughts. As we say these affirmations, we must visualize those things to be true. We must imagine and try to feel how it would feel if those things were true. It is how we create our reality.

Here is how I practice it every day:

After my morning meditation and Gratitude journaling, I close my eyes and say my positive affirmations. I repeat each affirmation 3–5 times. As I say these affirmations, I imagine and feel them being true.

Some of my favourite affirmations are:

I love myself.

I am beautiful.

I am healthy – physically, mentally, and emotionally.

I am smart.

I love my body.

I love my hair.

I am focused.

I am productive.

I am loving.

I am humble.

I am kind.

I am compassionate.

I am enough.

There is no substitute for hard work. We have got to do what we have got to do. However, having a positive mindset while working on our goals makes the journey easier. We must remember to enjoy life.

One Fine Night

by Chetan Singh Manhas

One fine night
Two souls merged under the moonlight
And their journey seemed to be bright.
After seven years, they whispered one night
The decision of coming together was damn right.
Through endless chuckles and innumerable lock horns
Even today, her smile makes his downhearted day bright.

She came as the sunshine when he was in rain
And became the drug to his pain.
The trust, the loyalty, and the solicitude they had gained
Being together was the only fantasy in their heart and brain.
Distance was a taxing thing to endure
And it made both their hearts distraught.
But for their love and their promise, they fought
Which, in turn, strengthened their bond.
On the hard days, when they didn't know what to do
The only solution they found was to say, "I love you!"

The Dawn of Hope

by Rohit Agrawal

In the midst of the cold
And the New Year night
I met a girl
Who was beautiful and bright

I couldn't control myself
After seeing her delightful greet
My plan of spending the night with friends
Seemed to take a backseat

Random plans are the best, they say
There only stays eternal bliss.
We, too, planned for the campus tour
But destiny had something better than this

The more we came close
The more I fell for the 'rising sun'!
Finally, I decided to share my feelings
At the dawn of 2021

After having 8 shots in the night
I already was in the world of leap
Her mesmerising sparkle in the eyes
Had me lost and made me asleep.

10 minutes after, I woke up in haste
To come on knees for my future spouse
But devil's destiny has planned something else
It had been 4 hours since I was lying on my couch

'Tani' was her name, I searched and searched
Just to see failure pave my way
"Real love wins one day" is the saying
With which my heart beats every day.

The Month of May

by Malvika Sharma

On that particular day, in the month of May
I decided to break all shackles and explore life ahead
As I pulled the curtains apart, the sun kissed my cheeks, and its
warmth hugged me
A strange yet strong energy passed down my spine
I felt it in my bones, and as it went deeper to touch my soul
I embraced it like home.
The leaves of the lush green garden waved at me
Creating a wind that whispered,
"Embrace the felicific ephemerals coming your way."

And on that particular day, in the month of May
I drove through the roads unknown,
My eyes sparkling fearlessly
My tresses highlighting the streaks
A familiar aroma surrounding me
While the radio playing its best melodies
Out of the blue started a downpour
And the rainbow romanticised with my soul

My body all drenched and its thirst all quenched
Two cups of Nescafe and our first fruit punch
While heading to the next destination to find some lunch
"Bingo!" I said to Cajun cheese dumplings and your one sexy wink
Life put forth all the signs together in sync.
And on that particular day, in the month of May
I had deeper conversations with you
I wore my heart on my sleeve and found my flaws being accepted
perfectly
I went to explore this less-travelled path of love a little more
And dive in the ocean of love and reach the shore
I decided all of it on that particular day
As I had met you, a man so suave!

You filled my life with nothing but love
You made me believe in the signs of the universe,
The signs of your love, the signs of our love,
And without you, I could have never had
A better day in the month of May!

You Are My Only Home

by Shabnam Islam

Can I tell you something?
How you brought me back to life?
When I lost hope and all seemed a lie,
You came in like a basking ray
Somewhere through the clouds.
Brought my smile back to my face
And love in my dying heart.
You really don't know how much you mean to me
Nor can I explain how...
Because words become short
when I see those Beautiful brown eyes,
Never knew what love was until I knew you,
Believe me my love you are more than this heart can beat.
The only beautiful thing I could ever have in my life,
Which not only pushes me to be strong
But to believe in myself.

I can't thank you more nor can I thank less,
You've become my heartbeat
Which throbs with every passing dawn of sunset.
I need not any promises to stay with me
Nor do I want any riches which are only make believe.
I just want what we have the never-ending trust
Because I can't ask for anything else who is mere a beggar at last!

Triumphant Crusades

by Mansha Kapoor

1 Year Ago

We both looked at each other for one last time before he left the apartment. He was wearing my oversized yellow mango hoodie, and those old jeans I loved so much. His dishevelled hair smelled of rich Park Avenue, and his eyes were a warm chocolate brown, with a tinge of red around them. The box had his books, laptop, and wallet in it.

"So, this is it," he said before closing the door behind him. He gave me a last crooked smile as if it was a peace flag and hugged me one last time. It was that moment I wanted to take in every millisecond I had left with him, rewind to the day we met, go back to the day we moved in together and do things differently just so we wouldn't part ways today, just so he wouldn't leave today. But he did.

I stared at the door for a long time, hoping he would come back, wishing he would text me just to say he loved me and couldn't stay without me. After four hours of sitting on the cold floor, and getting a butt ache, I finally gave up. I got up to make myself a hot cup of black coffee. I don't even like coffee, but he made me a cup every time I was sad. He used to say it elevates the mood and uplifts spirits. Wanting to drown in a pool of coffee, I poured myself a cup and sat on one of the red barstools we had bought together, just because "they looked cute". The coffee tasted horrible, but somehow it stopped the tears, like always.

Loneliness surrounded me, as the memories of the previous year flooded back to me.

1 Year 3 Months Ago

The house was in shambles. Glass shattered across the floor and clothes torn. The post-war remains included two red-eyed adults and the mist of shame and regret.

I was on a call with my two best friends, in the middle of a full-fledged rant about how unlucky I was to land with such an inconsiderate and selfish man, when I saw him across the room, frozen. I glanced at him and continued bitching about him. I wanted to hurt him so bad. I wanted to make him feel the pain I had felt in the last week, so I kept unravelling our deepest secrets to my girls. None of them stopped me, they kept criticising him, calling him names, and he just stood there listening. At one point, I saw his eyes welling up.

What is it with relationships? At one point you want to stab them with your words, the other second you want to hold them so close, so no one can hurt them. I never understood what happened to me when he and I used to fight. We would be in the middle of a break-up when I would just get up and go hug him tightly.

We would often talk about taking a break, maybe living away from each other for a few days to gain perspective. But it never happened. The thought of losing each other scared us. We would just forget everything that made us fight, and surrender. The thought of being away from each other, even for a day made us reconcile and get over the fight. What could we do? We were in love.

Even after many warnings from the girls to not go back to 'the jerk', I hung up and ran towards him to hug him tight. I could not bear to hurt him for a minute longer. I was done. I made it my sole purpose in my life to make him happy, and be the best girlfriend there ever was.

The resolution lasted for 3 hours before we started fighting again.

1 Year 2 months ago

It was 7 a.m., and instead of reading the daily news and enjoying their mundane cup of tea and biscuits, our neighbours were knee-deep into overhearing "that brazen couple" fight, while gossiping concomitantly.

The war lasted for 5 hours and ended with both parties surrendering and blocking their exes from every social media platform and call list.

I knew that she was a free soul when I met her, and I know she is a free soul now. But not being able to let go of her clingy ex and giving him the liberty to drunkenly call her is something I just can't understand. I sometimes feel she's still not over him. That hulk hurt her badly and she's still nice to him. And in return, I am sure he tells her she deserves someone better than me – maybe him again.

I sometimes feel I am not good enough for her, maybe that's why she still talks about her past. I have been her boyfriend for a long time now, but there is only so much I can take. She keeps saying I am not romantic enough, and I agree, I don't understand the need to be cringingly romantic like in the movies. My idea for a date is us sitting at home and watching sci-fi together.

Yesterday, she started a fight with me just because I wouldn't take her out for dinner on a Friday date night. I just don't see why I should act like those rom-com jokers, trying to make her feel special. She should know she's special without me having to prance around in suits, being sickly cheesy all the time.

She does look beautiful wearing that dress, I thought to myself sitting across the table, sipping wine while looking at her chatting with the waiter about the day's specials. I could live for that smile. I promised myself to take her out for a date every weekend if that's what it took to make her happy.

1 Year Ago

It was a series of such pending fights, unresolved issues and frustration that brought us to this doomed day; the day when we couldn't bear to be with each other any longer; the day when no number of tears could stop us from parting ways. We had crossed a threshold, from where it was impossible to return to what we used to be. Maybe we had fallen out of love, and maybe love was lost somewhere in these little battles we fought day in and day out. It was the day we finally realised we were never meant to be. The nagging, the disappointment and the misunderstanding of each other's emotions had led us to a level where we could no longer bear to be with each other anymore.

When I saw him leave, I knew he had taken a piece of my heart with him. A part of me, my identity and my personality had walked away through that door, waddling behind him waving goodbye to me. I knew I will never be the same. I feared the change, I feared the heartbreak. I was scared of not knowing what was in store for me. I desperately wanted to run after him, cling to him and bring back everything I had left 4 hours ago. At one time I even ran to the door to beg him to come back. So many backspaced texts, but I didn't dare to hit send on even one.

5 Months Ago

"I am still not ready to date anyone, yaar," I said while sipping my third cup of black coffee. I was trying to convince my best friend why I didn't want to accompany her on this double date she had been dreaming for about 3 weeks.

"You have been crying about him for months, you need to get back out there," she begged while devouring her Caesar salad. Brutus would have been proud.

Successfully getting my frustrated friend off my back, I crawled back home to my dark and empty apartment. Replaying 'the fight' in my mind for the 800th time, I made myself a coffee and sat down in front of Star Trek. It had become the background noise I used to sleep in. And sure enough, I drowsed off after a long day, envying the emotionless Mr. Spock all the way.

Today

Everyone has insecurities. Everyone at some point in their lives doubts their worth, their capabilities and their decisions. I happened to be fighting with mine for the past three years. Three years of self-doubting, of being under confident of thinking, looks, my abilities and myself.

I used to think all my insecurities would go away if I had a perfect relationship and the perfect guy. I always used to picture a knight in shining armour, coming to save me from the evil witch and my insecurities; on his horse and we would live happily ever after.

I got what I wished for, a real relationship, two years ago. But my insecurities never took the flight to the Bermuda Triangle. He wasn't the knight in shining armour I wanted him to be. My insecurities grew over time. I lost my true self somewhere between those lines, those months. But I couldn't understand what was happening, because I was too busy trying my best to believe that yes, it's all perfect, and yes, I was happy. I wasn't. I realised this when I finally let go.

Those fights were not about us. It was about me. I had changed into a person I didn't recognise. I wanted someone to appreciate me, take me out, plan dates for me, and think of me all the time. He was no longer my partner. I had become emotionally dependent on him, latching my insecurities onto him, expecting him to shoo them away from me. If only I had told him.

I was scared to let him go, not because I loved him but because I was scared to live a life without him. I would panic at the thought of losing him; the unsolicited memories of our little battles would make me shudder. Every time I got insecure, I would hold on to him a little tighter, try to make him stay a little longer. He was my shield against those uncertainties and more.

I don't blame him for walking away. Not anymore. He wasn't familiar with this version of me, and I never opened up to him about it. I just wanted him to know everything, read my mind and have the right thing to say each time.

And when he couldn't give me what I wanted, I would fight.

The little battles were not those that I was fighting against him, it was what we were fighting against my inner demons. My love had dissolved and changed into clingy reliance and a constant need for reassurance that I could not comprehend.

The breakup felt like being set free. I was finally free of my dependence. It was like leaving an anchor behind. I worked at changing myself. I struggled to find my happiness buried amid the fictional shattered glass and shambled home.

I wondered and wondered, retrospecting all my past mistakes, pondering over my relationship and my craving for him. *I needed him in my life, but I was not happy when he was in it.*

That's when it finally hit me, the knight in shining armour, on a horse, coming to save me was never supposed to be him. It was always me.

Part III

~ From escaping to embracing,
From doubting to believing,
From worrying to living ~

Autumn Roads

by Kruttika R. Hegde

Looking back at this journey
A long winding path,
So lonely, going on to an end
nobody can see,
A deep breathe in to fill some courage
Into a wildly beating heart
Turning to look at the journey
Far into the distant past
And slowly, those memories, they fall into place
Like Auburn leaves from flaming trees
Covering the path, a multitude
Of reds and oranges
Bright moments of days gone by
A look upon them and a smile
Finding the will to go on ahead
Through long autumn roads
Through weak sunshine
And into the starry night.

Balance Sheet

by Rinku Tyagi

Spring cleaning the house,
Quite a few days before the last
I dared to unburden my closet
Holding the reminiscent of the past,
And wiped the dust off,
Of fleeted, transited time
It was buried under,
For no reason or rhyme.

What did I find?

Stack of worn-out garbs,
Glimpse of birthday cards
Clink of few coins old,
Concealed by coats of mould
A gifted postcard faded
Some magazines jaded

Few dry petals frayed and coloured
Trapped between pages
Of personal memoir, crumpled
Lots of hazy memories, of candid random clicks

A sassy butterfly clip and two red lipsticks.
A long-lost key, one broken mirror
An odd fob chain,
Jewels in a box, silver.
Treasures stashed away
Buried, forgotten spectres of the past
Wadded and thrown
Wafting on the wings of air
Came instantly alive,
Like reels of a Polaroid
Strutting before my eyes.

My mind adjusting finally
To make room for old,
Familiar, near and dears
Tallied the income of joy
With the expenditure of tears
And prepared the balance sheet
Of all the painful, nostalgic years.

Loss of strength, gain of afflictions.
Subtraction of health, sound
Addition of a few extra pounds.
Damage of mental faculty
Building up of obscurity.
Increase in couth, decrease in youth.
Appearance of greys, disappearance of haste.
Securing experience, damage of negligence.
Depreciation of beauty, appreciation of ingenuity.

Monetary loss, profit of love
Investment in relations, returns of close connections.
Reckoning of the facts, meticulously arranged
In separate columns, perfectly managed.
Computing the addition and subtraction,
Profit and loss of various factions,
Facets of my mental acuity dwelled upon a decision.
The summation of happiness and negation of sorrow
Both were in uncanny distribution.
Fact remains that each moment
I spent in mirth or exasperation
Added to my personal reserve, and a
Sum total of everything, fairly and squarely
Made me what I am, in completion.

Down the Memory Lane

by Raghav Mahajan

A divine cleansing of a new life
In the heavenly skies
As the spirit rises to God
While we mortals blindly watch
The lowering of the casket
The rain clouding our eyes
Bringing forth the smell of the earth
Reminding us why we are here and
What this world has given us:
Life!
So, take a trip down the memory lane
And cherish every moment of it.

Firefly's Furry Friend

by Aditi Rao

On a cold night, a strong wind blows,
The firefly buzzes, her darkness shows,
She looks at the beaver and instantly knows,
That life is darker in the deep burrows.

He sends her back to the bright beginning,
Of smiles, of laughter or birds singing,
The river flows in you, he hopefully cries,
You shine when you burn, you don't simply die.

He paints a picture, simple yet compelling,
For her to see; the real, the telling,
To struggle and judgement, he is not a stranger,
Yet battles he wins, like a skilful ranger.

The firefly dances, ready to shine,
She's glad she's high; no worry, no whine,
She heads for the burrows, to lighten the dark,
As long as she shines, in the corner she larks.

Why should she be ordinary? To burn, to die?
She'll dance with the beaver, she wouldn't comply,
To wishes of nature, the world, the lie,
Life is a tug; you win, or you tie.

She'll chart a new way, for light in the darkness,
They will co-exist in their glory, their starkness,
Hope is real, not an ideal to jade,
She will brighten the darkness, not simply fade.

After years you'll see, how the burrows will bloom,
With light, with songs, no sadness, no gloom,
Painted with unicorns and dripping with honey,
The life they lead will be simple and funny.

Fleeting Moments

by Rinku Tyagi

A moment of joy
An instance of bliss
Overwhelmingly pure
Too good to miss.

A wisp of charm
A freckle of innocence
An ounce of love
Bubbling effervescence.

Precious moments
Priceless and tender
Joy immeasurable
To us they render.

A silent applaud
A loud cheer
A warm hug
Of someone close and dear.

A chat with friends
To your heart's content
Meaningless gossip
With no reason or intent.

A sip of coffee
On a cool rainy day
Reading a book
Keeps worries at bay.

Foggy morning
Makes you snuggle
Happy sunshine
Leaves a chuckle.

Tranquil silence
Fluttering thoughts
Each is special
Aimless, they're not.

Tears of joy
A hearty laughter
Unburdens your heart
Makes it lighter.

Timeless, fleeting, wee moments
Leave a trail indelible around
String of these cherished pearls
Adorn life with mirth abound.

From Perfection to Peace

by Mohammed Sadiq

Unparalleled creation
With the ability to perceive
Beauty in every little thing
But in themselves

Multifarious generations
Learnt and taught the art
Of gratitude for everything
But in themselves.

With faulty lineage comes
A perfectly imperfect soul
Who knows to be flawless
But never was.

Forged in hell for years
With every negative etiquette
Forcing to be brute savage
But never was

Neither excelled nor failed
In the arduous walk of life
Only to be humiliated often
But realised it's alright.

Eluded from human feelings
Preferring on one's own
Not loved or ever been in one
But realised it's alright.

Comprehending the reality
Chaos in order, evil in good
Is not to be anxious of
But is impeccable.

Through thick and thin
The only constant is oneself
Is not to be wretched of
But is impeccable.

Learning the new norms
The imperfect soul is happy
Without excitement
But finally, in peace.

Here I Am

by Vanshika Gupta

Eagerly waiting for the new beginnings
Where every beginning is just another end
A loop that traps me inside
Suffocating me enough to lose my vision
Where am I?
The ideal notion in my mind
Blurs my will
To roam around with open arms
I search through the pieces
Reaching the destination, but almost
Somewhat delighted by the world so great
Locating my footsteps again
Then what keeps me grounded?
The thought of not having this otherwise
Perfection is an illusion
I alert myself
Reminiscing the happier times
Trying to assimilate the trajectory
Of reaching the almost

Here I am,
Far from perfect
Regretting my ways
But, in the frenzy of moments
Through the sunlight and the rain
I made it to this very moment
By believing into my reality
A little blurry
And the only perfect it could be.

In Every Breath

by Shay P. Kris

Hope is just a four-letter word,
Which holds so much power.
Not just for you but me as well,
I feel it in every breath I take.

I feel it every morning,
And every night.
For my night to turn to day,
For light to shine away the dark.

I dream hopelessly
For better days.
For brighter tomorrows,
For fate to show me my path.

I seek greatness,
And greatness I shall find.
Come hell or high water,
I will not stop.

I beseech you to join me,
To find your greatness.
To find your dream,
And make this world great again.

The world was great before,
And it can be great again.
Join hands with each other,
And we will achieve greatness together.

Love Beyond Words

by Ashyl Elizabath Paul

Romantic movies! They are something that I love watching all the time. Right from my childhood, every time I saw them, it became difficult for me to get over those beautiful happy endings, through all the drama and the chaos. The happily ever after depicted in these movies had me craving to live even a bit of such lives and stories. Someone who would drag me by my feet and making me fall head over heels for him, someone who would care for me when I was upset or sick, someone who would get angry with me for my carelessness and someone who would love me more than anyone in this whole wide world; even though I knew that it was all far away from reality. In reality, things are very different. If you love someone, the universe will not show the signs. And for sure, it will neither rain nor snow when your soul mate will walk past you. And so, the chances of you being able to hear your rising heartbeat when you see 'the one' will be quite low due to the ever-increasing roadway noise.

However, there was this time in my life these movies had gotten in my head for real and I had just fallen for this guy, thinking that the whole universe is giving me the signs. This happened when I was in college. One day after the class was over, my friends and I, as usual, were leaving the campus; there was this guy, who was a friend of one of my friends. He came close to us, and all of a sudden, stopped and started talking to her. When I saw his face, a wind blew on to my face and the surroundings became colder, exactly like in the movies. I felt like everything around me had faded and it was just him in front of me. Oh, my God! What was that feeling? I just kept thinking about it while getting onto the bus and reached home.

I couldn't sleep that night, thinking about who he really was and which department he belonged to. Hours later, the sun was out, and I ran and got ready for college. At the college entrance, I waited for this friend of mine to whom he had spoken to. You might be thinking that in a modern era like this, when we have phones, why did I just not text or call her and ask her for his name and details the other day? It would have saved time as well. But I was in love, that too, love at first sight, and I was dumb. I waited a while and then realized that I was late and she might have gone to her class, so I ran to her class, caught hold of her and asked her for his details. Only if destiny weren't that harsh, she had no idea who I was talking about. She was staring at my face all blank, wondering whether it was a real encounter, or I was just daydreaming!

Later, I saw him in the afternoon, thanks to the universe. To be frank, the whole college knew him because he was taking part in some fest promotion. That is when I ran to my friend and told her I was talking about this particular guy, and she told me his name and department along with the semester because that was important for me to know as I didn't want to date someone younger than me (and disappoint my family in the future based on the traditions and customs of our society). So yes, she introduced me to him and because of my big mouth, all my friends, in the sense, our entire gang ultimately got to know about my feelings for him. This gave way to my increasing frustration as now the entire college knew, and I couldn't do anything about it. Just imagine how dramatic it was that he called me personally to ask about the spreading chaos and confusion and I couldn't utter a word.

Then after waiting for, I guess one month, I got his number from my friend after promising her that I wouldn't text him, but one day, I lost all my patience and just went ahead and texted him. However, I lied to my friend that it was by mistake, because I knew she cared for me and would have killed me for dragging myself into this mess, again. So, I texted him and then, we started talking casually, and after some time, I finally gathered the courage and told him what I felt for him. And to my surprise, he said that he knew it from day one from the way I was acting around him. Speechless and thoughtless, only if I could hide in my closet for eternity! However, he didn't say anything about what he felt back for me. I was curious to know but was just as scared of getting rejected. He was typing. I sat in one place, biting my nails and fingers crossed, wishing he would say that he felt the same. But he didn't. He said, "You are an amazing person, and you deserve the best." The first thought that came into my mind was that if I do, why is it not you? I was so disappointed and upset that I cried and cried for days.

I lost my self-confidence. I did not want to see his face again. I was embarrassed and started doubting myself, thinking that only if I would have been more beautiful and modish like the other girls, maybe then he would have felt something for me. But still, I was determined. I thought I should try and convince him. Maybe it was the fear of acceptance or the pain of rejection; I went to such an extent, questioning my worth and keeping my self-respect at stake that he literally stopped talking to me. I started hating myself. Ashamed and disappointed, I wanted to get rid of my existence. I had lost all my confidence and even tried getting a complete makeover, but I was not that well off to do it. I was devastated.

Though we don't realize, rejection does make us vulnerable. We don't know what we end up doing when we are not accepted the way we are. There are so many people who just ended their life because they were not able to cope up with this pain. I wanted to do that as well. Though I knew that everyone has their own right to decide, I was still not ready to accept that decision of his. I only thought that the sole reason for all of this is my appearance that I couldn't think straight for a long, long time.

Now, after all these years when I sit and think about how far I have reached, I am glad that I had the courage to overcome it and become a stronger person. Today, if someone else rejects me as well, I won't be that upset, because I know that the fault is not in me. Love is like this; not all lovers have their love reciprocated. What's important today is that I love myself and that is all that matters.

The most foolish thing we can do with ourselves is doubt our self-worth in such circumstances. It's not at all easy to live in these times without confidence and courage. And there is one thing we as humans should always remember, that no matter how different we may be, we are all beautiful in our own unique ways. Only when we love ourselves first do we see love coming back to us in so many ways.

So, get up stronger and wiser, for you are worth all the good things that this world has to offer.

Just Breathe

by Kruttika R. Hegde

Little eyes dream, stars littering the deep blue
And this little body trembles, containing the hurricane
Is no easy feat
Come for once, let us taste
Just a bite of freedom
For once, with no care for scrutiny
Let out the majestic beast you hide inside your soul
You carry this burden so well
On those capable shoulders
But for once, let it fall away
This need to please
For once just breathe.

Kindness: A Weapon to Strive

by Raghav Mahajan

Nowadays, being kind is a rarity
These days to love is considered a rebellion
So, if to be kind and to be loving is dissent
My dear,
You be the rebellion
You be the opposition
You be the resistance
Be part of the uprising
Be part of the revolt.

Life in a Cup of Tea

by Angela Sharon

What is the morning without a single cup of tea?
How dreary my day would be without a single cup?
Each sip I take recites a tale of its own.

The first sip makes my teeth grit
The flash of pain reminding me of the sorry world I live in
The pain is fleeting but the memory remains.

The second sip after a careful blow
Now as I reach this point in life
I hold my guard up high
Taking each step slower than before.

The third sip is slightly cooler now
I become resilient to all
Taking each step forward steadily.

The fourth sip which I'm yet to take
Knowing that peace is brief
I'm yet to lower my guard
Taking each step cautiously now.

The fifth sip I hardly feel
I've fought valiantly and returned victorious from the fight
Now taking each step with pride.

As I take my final gulp
I reminisce how I fought my battles
Taking each step with my head held high.

With each sip of the piping hot tea
I think of the long way I've come
Taking each step in a stride as I go.

What would my day be without a cup of tea?
To tell me a story of my own.

Musing

by Rinku Tyagi

Refreshing gale rubs its soothing palm
Against my coloured cheeks
Few strands of my truant tresses
Reeling about my unflustered face

My physical being resting calmly
In the ninth zenith of complacency
Sleep has robbed my senses of the ability to prompt response or
reason.

Mind unfazed by even the bleakest suspicion of the impending
scorch
The overzealous and raging time may subject it to, eventually.

Notion of the omnipresent turmoil
Or immediate urge for achievement
Leave no mark of its presence
In the rapturous meadow
Of my conscious, waking self.

What matters most, in the
Irrevocable splendour of this fleeting moment
Is to banish the din of chaos and clamour
And absorb the serenity and wonder of nature.

Of Man and Mortal

by A. Prakruthi

The day cruise is iffy,

Let one's tresses down,

As the stage is ready to open out over,

Give a hat tip to the author!

Every mortal is just like a spot of ink in a pot,

Waiting, to commit to writing,

In a stony leaf,

On today's date.

Our soul and we sap as odds-on,

But we endure polarity,

We fancy a day's brightness,

The sphere is a myth,

But the esse is a fantasy,

When thou whirl thy era,

Wend thou way through the woodland,

To get a glimpse of the briny,

To get a whiff of Zephyr,

While away rhythm is spesh,

Every whilom day is excogitated.

Times never hammered out,
Freedom of doubt is a relief,
Forfeiting a bird is grief,
But when a new smirk is vouchsafed,
A state-of-the-art of new floret,
A beaut feat will flourish into a credo,
And never be a dead widow.

The Crown You Wear

by Vanshika Gupta

A little bit of highs
A little bit of lies
Running to the hills
Chasing the kites
Smiling and scared
Playing with fears
Catching up with all
Let bygones be bygones.

Never giving up
Strengthening goals
Finding happiness in small kinds
Empathy for every kind
What's right and what's wrong?
Partially informed of every sort
A drop in the ocean
Cleansing the whole.

Bit by bit
Working for the good
Good to better
Better to best
Endlessly thriving until the end
Descending negatives
Hoping for a clear sky.
A little bit of shade
A little bit of light
Task to the shallow
Life to the profound
Learning till eternity
Well deserving of the crown.

The Peace Within

by Rakhee Daryanani

Take a slow breath, oh, dear human!
The world will go at its own pace
Your health is yours and yours alone
Worrying about the world will leave you torn.

Take a gentle breath, oh, dear human!
You need the peace within your soul
The beauty of sanity lies within you
Pull it out and spread it with others too.

Take a pause, oh, dear human!
Move a step back and reflect on yourself
The world is rushing, but you stay in peace
Do not stress yourself; find a method of stress release.

Take a calm breath, oh, dear human!
The beauty of peace deserves to unfold
To all the creatures that are out there forlorn
Live and let live for the world is ours and ours alone.

Walk by Faith

by Varun Ahuja

My first profession was not by choice, but the second one, I will always be proud of.

I remember that day I woke up in the morning and as per routine, my father and I went farming. On our way to the farm, he always used to teach me some great moral lessons and for that day his lesson was, "Prashant, we people might be counted as low-class families, but we have a major contribution to our country's development; never, ever underestimate the power of people like us in the future." I couldn't agree more with his words, but at the same time, I was concerned about one thing, that is, if we are a major contributor to the country's development, then why do we always have to struggle for our needs and rights? I knew that Bapu had the answer for this, but he was trying to present it in a more relatable and understandable manner to me.

In the midst of it all, he felt an acute pain in his chest, and the next moment, he fainted. I was in utter shock and had no idea of what I should have done in that appalling circumstance. We were lucky, though, that around 2–3 farmers were nearby, and they took him to a government hospital in the village. He was admitted to the emergency ward, and outside the room, there was chaos in my mind while my surroundings felt numb. All I could hear was my voice praying for my Bapu's speedy recovery and well-being. After about half an hour, the doctor came out and told us that he was now fine, but he had a minor heart attack and needed to get bed rest for a couple of months. This news brought me a great sigh of relief that he was now out of danger, but at the same time, I was concerned because he was the only breadwinner in the family. This was the time the responsibility was on me, and so, I started farming on my own. I did it for a month, but I wasn't able to make enough money out of it as I was not well experienced.

It was a regular evening when we got a call from Raju Uncle who lived in Delhi and had called to ask about Bapu's well-being. Over the call, he suggested that I should come to Delhi and work for his company. Maa and Bapu didn't have much discussion over it as we were not left with any other option at that time, and we all thought that it was rather a good idea to make ends meet for our family. That's where my journey started.

I was so excited with the thought that I was now going to work in an urban area without worrying about the difficulties that this sudden and extreme change in area and surroundings would bring for me. I left for Delhi on the 15th of August 2019 from my hometown, Khuri, Rajasthan. It was around 22 hours of a wearing journey. The bus dropped us at the local bus station, and I got off with one bag of luggage and an abundance of excitement. On my way, Uncle had called to inform me that he would be waiting for me there at the bus station, and luckily, I found him at a small tea shop.

We took a rickshaw to reach his residence, and that first Delhi ride was good enough for me to explore and experience the city life. There was a lot to see and absorb with no end to my amusement and exuberance. There were people nicely dressed up, heading towards their destinations in big luxurious cars. The malls, like I had never seen before, were profound with hundreds of shops and restaurants inside them. Riding past these buildings, I wondered if there are schools and other educational institutions like these, too, and how good it would be to have even a bit of such quality infrastructure in our village. There were cinemas, hotels, circuses, gardens, hospitals, and everything that you would need as a necessity or for entertainment.

We were about to reach but then got stuck in a traffic jam. I had only heard from the news about the much devastating 'Delhi's traffic and pollution'; that day, I witnessed it too and the chaos spoiled the good time I was having while exploring the city. In the middle of this, a cute little girl child came to us and was trying her best to sell some key chains. Uncle was busy on a call; I liked one of the key chains and bought it from her for 60 rupees. Trust me, that smile on her face relieved all my anguish from hearing those irritating honks and roars. Finally, we reached his residence and post-lunch and some rest, we headed to his office where I was introduced to other employees, where one of them was asked to make me understand the work process and my role there.

Uncle Raju was the main supplier of an electronic brand in that area, and it took around 15-20 days for me to get settled and start working there as a back-office person. Everything was going well; it had been 2 months since I was working there. Out of my office hours, I took Uncle's permission for exploring the city. I bought a saree for Maa and a shirt for Bapu from a local shop, and I decided to send them these gifts along with my monthly income. It had become a routine for me to start my day with a morning walk and then having breakfast before the office and visiting the market post-office.

On 3rd of December, we received a legal notice at Uncle's office, in which it was written that because of some legal issue, the company had to stop its operations till further notice. Uncle Raju went insane at this notice as it had taken him 8 years to build this business. We all were worried about our jobs while Uncle was visiting the lawyer's office to get this issue resolved as soon as possible; the lives of so many people including him were at stake due to the sudden shutdown. Uncle finally got a lawyer who was ready to fight the case, but it was informed by the court that in the meantime, the company had to stop its operations completely.

As the court was now involved in this case, he suggested everyone to start searching for another job as we had no idea how much time it would take to start the business again. Like other employees, I was suggested the same thing. Now, the problem for me was that I had been in Delhi for just 4–5 months, and hence, I had no knowledge of how to approach these companies for a job. Rakesh, whom I had met at Uncle's office, was now a good friend of mine and he helped me in searching for companies, prepared me for the interviews, and taught me the basics. Because of him, I did appear for multiple interviews but wasn't selected by any of them, because of my low experience and confidence in the corporate sector.

I even tried to apply at local shops, food stalls but while some were searching for well-experienced staff, some didn't have the capacity of employing even a single worker. This process was too time-consuming, and it was necessary for me to start earning again, as I needed to send money to my family for their daily expenses including the additional expenditure of medicines. In the meantime, I remembered that little girl who was independently selling key chains on the roads. I went to the signal, which was near Uncle's house, and saw a group of 5–6 people who were selling strawberries, car and bike accessories, wallets, mobile accessories, and many other things. I asked them if I could also join their business. They were confused and after explaining to them my entire situation, they told me that they were not one group; rather they all were selling the products independently. One of them even helped me set my block up and as per his guidance, I decided to start selling pens, pencils, and key chains. I purchased 20 products each and a board to hang them.

Like them, I used to sell at signals, over the roads but realised that it was not as easy as it seemed. From 50 of them, you would just have 2–3 customers who would buy these products, and that, too, after bargaining. I knew that I could make money from here, but not as per the requirement. I didn't face much difficulty getting another job as I was now connected with some people who had good contacts. I discussed this with them and one of them introduced me to Samid Chacha who was a local city cleaner. He was good and polite. I met him and after talking with the administration, he got me a job with enough pay.

Initially, I was full of apprehension about doing this job, but then decided to go with it. My life slowly started coming back to track. Time passed, it was March 2020, and I was juggling 2 jobs in Delhi while not being able to generate much money from selling products on roads, but having good work as a local city cleaner. It was tough to do this work, like when you started with the AC office, a chair, and a computer, and now you were directly selling products to customers and working as a city cleaner. But every work becomes doable for you when you have responsibilities on your shoulder.

As the time passed, and the country was made aware of Covid-19, the Prime Minister announced a nationwide lockdown for 7 days. It was notified that no one will step out of their homes and all offices and shops had to remain closed for 7 days. I was worried and went to Samid Chacha about this concern. He said that the city cleaners' work was not going to stop, and we would be getting paid for that. I was happy to hear that as I knew my keychain and pen selling business was going to pause for a week due to lockdown. Unfortunately, the situation was getting worse, and people were getting unimaginably affected by the virus. To control it and as a measure of safety, the lockdown was extended for the next few months.

We as city cleaners were also at high risk and were working relentlessly with masks on our faces and sanitizers in our pockets. In the meanwhile, I contacted Maa and Bapu to know how they were doing and made them aware of the spreading virus and how to take precautions for the same. Despite this dangerous situation, as some of us were still working for the nation, the PM in one of his speeches addressed us as the "Front Line Warriors of the country". That was the time I remembered Bapu's lesson about the importance of our contribution to our country. Yes, Bapu, you were right.

One of the happiest moments for me was when the interviewer came to us and took our picture which was published in newspapers and was also shown on television. With this month of pay, I happily sent our picture to Maa and Bapu saying that I was proud of all that I was doing there.

Today, thinking of every little thing that made me who I am and writing about my growth and change in perception of this world, I feel nothing but pride and gratitude. While most of us have some or other fancies to fulfil, some of us find it hard to even fulfil our necessities; but those who find their purpose even in the darkest of times and never let go of the faith in the Almighty and themselves, live the life they were meant to be and not just destined to be. So, what are you waiting for?

Live it, make it, and own it!

The Race

by Rinku Tyagi

A part of life, I have lived
A part, still lingers
A long way, I have covered
Much longer, still matters.

What is the destination?
Nobody cares to ask.
A never-ending road
And endless errands and tasks.

Weary of the ceaseless run
If I stop and rest
The world seems rushing by
Marching ahead; at behest?

Looking back, I descry
Joy abounds in smallest of things,
Numerous such moments alike
Left behind to spread some wings.

Still on the run, I struggle
Dishevelled by the pace,
Wary of the consequences
Of the never-ending race.

The Rising Sun
(Companion to 'The Setting Sun')

by C.L.Y.

Visualise witnessing the rising sun,

Standing, solitary, statue-still on a beach,

The waves caressing your buried feet.

The golden rays of our star brighten the skies above,

Shining out from beyond the thick curtain of concealing clouds,

As the birds sweetly rejoice the elimination of darkness,

And the silver crescent moon sets beyond the skyline.

The foliage rustles in the breeze,

Refreshing itself with a new rush of energy.

The waters celebrate as well by lightening up,

Going from azure to aqua within a few precious moments.

All life awakens to begin anew,

For this is a new dawn, a new hope,

As the sun rises every day without obligation,

Reminding us that the darkness must vanish,

And that the darkest nights must open gateways to the brightest
sunrises.

Experiencing the grandeur of this moment,
The golden sun rising out from beyond the horizon,
Something sparks up within –
A stimulation of inner passion,
A stirring up of fresh hope,
The unfamiliar feeling of euphoria surging through,
Enhancing joy and admiration,
And enlightening the mind, now ablaze with inspiration.
One day,
When all is said and done,
We will all shine brightly,
Our radiance engulfing this large yet small planet,
Inspiring many other beams of light, each so unique,
Just like the spectacle before our eyes does so every day –
The wondrous phenomenon of the rising sun.

The Setting Sun

(Companion to 'The Rising Sun')

by C.L.Y.

Visualise witnessing the setting sun,

Standing amidst many others on a high, hustling hill,

The wind ensuring that your hair doesn't sit still.

The golden rays of our star get dimmer by the moment,

As it sets further and further, signifying the long day's end,

As the birds quieten to welcome their time of much-needed rest,

And a luminous full moon shines out from behind you.

The rustling flora settles as the wind stills,

Bringing about an aura of peace all around.

The night sky opens up to the naked eye,

Revealing a thousand spectacular stars, sparkling and stunning.

All life prepares to rest and refresh,

For this is a soothing and calming twilight,

As the sun sets every day when its time comes,

Reminding us that nothing in life is permanent,

And that darkness and light are inevitable parts of something
whole.

Experiencing the stillness of this moment,
The fiery sun disappearing from beyond the horizon, beyond your sight,
Something settles deep inside –
A heartfelt appreciation for the calmness,
A newly kindled emotion of wholeness,
The wonderfully heavy feeling of peace around and within,
Igniting deeper comprehension of the necessity of endings,
And embracing the beauty of the new beginnings they bring.
On some nights,
In the unavoidable future,
We will all be surrounded by the darkness,
And amidst that darkness, we will understand,
How vital it is to life that the day doesn't stay permanently,
And why day must give rise to the beautiful nighttime every now and then,
And so, it does, every night – with the tranquil setting sun.

The Selfless Parachute

by Neeraja Krishnaswami

Life is timed,
Yet, we don't let it go.

Life is all about mishaps,
Yet, we clutch on to it, more.

Greatness is nothing before life,
And living is not a choice,
Just like we can't choose when we come or when we go.

Our actions and reactions reveal all about us,
Which, in turn, makes us rise or fall in our own eyes.

Neither do positives make our life simple,
Nor do negatives bring us down,
It is all about the vibe of life –
That we pour out.

We wait,
For the tide to recede.
Such times warrant us to become the parachute
Of an ailing life,
Of an inexplicable complication,
Of an endangering situation,
Rather than drowning in the expanse
Of guilt and self-pity.

Life and health go hand in hand,
It is a perspective in itself,
And life is worth living
If we are healthy, not wealthy.

Still, it is noteworthy
That striking a balance between the negative and positive,
Waiting for the tide to recede,
Is as important as becoming the parachute in one's life.
For, the same situation may engulf us all one day,
And preparation is the key.

Life is not a ballroom dance,
It is a harsh reality
That we need to face –
With sheer strength and will,
With undisturbed composure and golden silence,
With serenity and responsibility,
While living as a selfless parachute,
Voyaging in the lap of
Trust and faith.

Until the Sun Rises

by Angela Sharon

The sun rises from the east
People rise with the sun
Starting their day as the clock screeches at dawn.

They rise to start the day with joy
Loving the hustle, the day brings forth
The scorching heat brings them comfort and serenity.

Oh, why don't I share their joy?
Dreading the hustle and bustle
All day I'd grumble.

How I wait for the sun to set
For this tedious day to come to an end
As the sun sets my new day begins.

At night starts my day with joy
As I'm free without the hustle
I'm free to be me and to exhale in peace.

I abandon my worries
Stretching out every moment of my new day
Enjoying the silence with my symphonies.

My mind is clear as I gear up for the scorching glares again
Knowing that every slip hardens me
I strategize and remain unshakable.

I leave my troubles to tomorrow
Until the sun rises.

Where Life Lives

by Tashu Malik

That little space
Where the little bird
Perches atop
A tiny birdbath
To sing its tune
Oblivious to the din
Of the chaos around
That little nook
Where the potted bud
First wakes up
To yellow sunshine
Cheery and bright
Unheeding the concrete abound
All it takes is a little time
To find that space

Look for that nook
Where life really lives
Amid all that surrounds
For everyone
Deserves to have
A little sunshine
And their own very song.

Your Lighthouse

by Puja Bordoloi

The moon winks a sparkle,
With love and faith
For tranquillity to encircle,
Assuring of moving ahead,
And never to await.
Old gold melodies,
Of the cassettes,
Those treasured memories
Play amidst silent nights,
Make me suffer
Of acute nostalgia,
As well as frights.
Melancholy drains,
For the time,
Never repeats again.
Weaving beads of hope,
Breathing in positive thoughts
Adamantine, you see!
Oblivious of the cord.

I try to channelise my energies,
With the cosmos showering sanity
By my ears, gently the wind caresses
With the shrill swirling blow's sympathy.
While the tiniest star,
Strenuously speaks,
"Please wake up, I may fall asleep."
In complete darkness,
Its beauty enhances
But the dawn and its cruelty,
Persuades to glow faintly.
Compelled to live,
Learn and perceive
The gifts and griefs,
Appreciate while you breathe.

Every failure to rise,
From nothingness,
To an absolute being
Like a phoenix,
At the earliest hour
Spreading its wings,
Life can make us count
All the blessings,
And one's worth to surmount,
In taking back the broken pride
With confidence and satisfaction,
In knocking down barriers
For the soul to exclaim on death,
That "I lived, rather than just to exist"
Your Lighthouse, life ascertains.

The Lost Courier

by Rohan P. Lapalikar

2036

"Grade 9. One-day excursion to National Gallery of Modern Art" was written on the bus banner and the kids were not at all tired of all these games and chit chats. In the last row was Abhimanyu, sitting, listening to songs and busy in his own world.

'Abhi, Come, let's go,' said Vartika, his brilliant and beautiful twin sister.

Abhi rolled his sleeves up, flaunting a Shiva tattoo on his right forearm and hung his bag on one shoulder. As both got out of the bus post the instructions by the teacher, all students parted ways. As told by their parents, Vartika and Abhimanyu explored the art gallery together. Out of more than a thousand masterpieces, while exploring, Vartika came across a 3-foot canvas painting and as she went ahead to have a closer look, her eyes widened with shock. The painting had no signature.

'Abhi, just see this!' She called him.

2012

Aryana, a studious and an attractive girl, along with her friend Tarang sat three benches ahead of Bhargav. It was a physics lecture and Bhargav was already bored. As it ended, Bhargav, while packing up his bag, noticed that Aryana had forgotten to take her physics book back.

'Oh, God! There's a physics test tomorrow,' he murmured to himself.

Without any further delay, he grabbed her book and rushed to the station, but Aryana and Tarang had left. He stood at the station waiting for the next train, knowing where she was going to deboard. He spotted her right outside the station in the queue for a rickshaw.

'Aryana!' he shouted and ran towards her.

'Hey, Bhargav!' she was surprised upon seeing him.

'You… forgot…' he paused as he was panting. 'Your physics book. And tomorrow, we have a test.'

'Oh, my God! Thank you so much.' She was glad and felt short of words to thank him.

'It's okay. You don't have to thank me,' he smiled. 'But if I may ask something…'

'Sure!' she said.

'What does Aryana mean?' he asked.

'Seriously?' she replied with a strange look. 'It means desire or wish.'

'Oh! That's nice. I Aryana you.' he said softly, and she heard it.

'What?' she exclaimed and laughed before getting into the rickshaw.

'Go safe. See you tomorrow.' said Bhargav as he waved goodbye.

Aryana was excited and she narrated the whole incident to Tarang on Monday during class. Suddenly, a pen fell near Aryana's feet. It was Bhargav's pen, and he bent down to pick it up. It was a small gesture to make eye contact with her, but it was in vain. Aryana ignored his gestures but also enjoyed them. As the day ended, she forgot her biology textbook and expected him to return.

To his surprise, this time, she waited at the station.

'Hey, hi!' She greeted him by tucking her hair behind her ear.

Bhargav, as always, with a weird, confused smile, said 'Hi!'

'Did I miss something?' she asked.

'Yes, your biology book, Madam. May I ask something?' he said.

'Sure!' she said.

'Have you done a crash course in short-term memory loss?' he asked, smiling.

'No…' she paused. 'It's a talent,' she said, and they both laughed.

'Hey, why don't we exchange numbers, so the next time I forget something, you can call me, and I will wait for you here?' she asked with a mischievous smile.

It took a few seconds for Bhargav to digest it. 'Wow. That's a mind-blowing idea,' he nearly shouted, and they exchanged numbers.

A few months down, Bhargav found a study companion and a best friend in a single person. Both of them started liking each other. Being afraid of rejection, they never confessed their feelings. Knowing that they would have to part ways soon, they focused on their studies but spent the entire day talking.

It was March 2013, their exam was scheduled for May, and their preparatory leave started. Aryana being studious started to study vigorously and made a pact with him to not talk till their exams. Both turned their phones off while Aryana turned it on after a month to see if they could still talk, but it was in vain. Little did they know what was coming! Bhargav could not make it, but Aryana stood in merit. While she got into a government medical college, he was left with no option other than B.Sc.

Years passed by, and he missed her often. Both changed their numbers, so they could not contact each other. 5 years down the line, he completed his master's, and she was in her final year of MBBS. That was when he crossed paths with Tarang at a photography exhibition. Being a classmate of Aryana, she was also a doctor and a freelance photographer now. They followed each other on Instagram and through her following list, he followed Aryana and she followed him back immediately. Feelings blossomed in his heart again, and he cried with happiness. They both decided to meet over a coffee and share their current status of life and whereabouts.

To their shock, she had been in a toxic relationship while he had been in two. Knowing each other's pain, she consoled him and assured him that he was strong. She had moved on from him, thinking it was merely a school crush, but he still had an undying soft corner for her.

'What will you do now?' she asked.

He took a deep breath and said, 'Look for a stable job ASAP,' he replied, 'in a school probably, as a teacher. And you?'

'Studying for my masters; the entrance exam is in July,' she said.

Months later, Bhargav was a successful teacher in a secondary school while she was in Pune, studying first-year neurology. They were not in contact except through Instagram. During their busy lives, Bhargav got into a relationship with a classmate, but Aryana kept lingering in his mind for the next couple of years.

He broke apart from yet another relationship and finally decided to contact Aryana, but she didn't respond to his messages or calls. Later, she messaged him, and they started talking.

'Are you, okay?' he asked in a shivering voice.

'Yes, I guess!' she replied.

'What happened? You sound low.' he asked.

'Nothing, I am good.

After a pause, both said together, 'Just got out of a toxic relationship.'

'What?' he asked in shock, 'Again?'

'Yes. What was I supposed to do? Contain my feelings?' she said as she was about to cry.

'Okay, hold on. Let's not talk about this, ever. Deal?' He asked in a soothing tone.

She took a pause and said, 'Okay. Do you still like coffee?'

'Yes. I recently had Davidoff. And it was seductive,' he replied in a laughing tone.

'I know, right? That, too, black, without milk. It's seductive on a different level. What's your current favourite?' She asked.

And they started their happy conversation. Aryana felt very comfortable talking to him regularly and shared her problems, to which he sometimes tried to find solutions. One fine day, she showed him a few paintings that she had made in her free time. While browsing some supplies on Amazon, she saw a painting canvas and wanted to order it.

'Bhargav, listen.' she said over video call, 'I am sending you a screenshot. Should I purchase it?' she asked.

'Yes, sure,' he said after seeing the canvas. 'It's good. Go ahead. And what about a brush set?' he asked.

'I don't have one. But I think I can manage with a normal brush set as well.' she paused, 'Brush sets are expensive, and so is an oil paint set.'

Little did she know, half her address was visible in the screenshot. Bhargav saved it.

Days passed, and Bhargav still struggled to make her happy with his small gestures and sense of humour. Fed up with his vain efforts, he called her up.

'What is stopping you from being strong?' he asked in an affirmative tone.

'Nothing, I am fine,' she replied.

'You know what? Even I have problems in my life, Aryana. But I keep them aside when talking to you. Because I don't want to see you sad,' he said.

'Okay,' she replied.

'I,' he paused, 'I am not in the mood for small talk, and I truly care for you. Okay?'

'Bhargav, I know that. You are like a saint. I enjoy talking to you. I know I had feelings for you, but the situation has changed. I can never completely heal from what happened in my past. I have tried and failed miserably. I cannot go back to the person I was. And I beg you to please accept it,' she said in one go. Her agony was visible.

'I have accepted you and I am not trying to change you. I just want you to know that there is still hope for you to cherish and enjoy this life,' he replied in a soft tone.

'No, Bhargav. I have no hope for life or love. I am good at nothing except struggling hard and giving my exams.' She paused and there was utter silence between them. 'Bye. I will talk later.'

'Bye. Take care,' he said helplessly.

He was shattered as he could see his efforts going in vain again. He got no chance to tell her that he might be moving abroad next month and might not hear from her again. He gathered himself and wrote her a small letter. As he got busy with his shift to Canada and looking for a hostel, he was waiting for her reply as well. As he convinced himself that she wouldn't reply, he was about to delete his social media accounts and change his number. Tarang contacted him a few weeks later.

'Hey, dude. What's up? How is photography going on?' she messaged.

'Hey Tarang, how are you? Wasn't expecting your message,' he replied.

'I am good. Where have you been? It's been a long time,' she asked.

'No photography as of now. I am trying to isolate myself,' he took a pause, 'and life is good. Chances of getting better are always there. It's been a month since I have been in Canada.'

'Why are you being so closed off? You used to talk a lot.'

'It's a long story. May I ask you for a favour?' he asked.

'Yes, I guess.' she replied doubtfully.

'It's been almost 3 and a half weeks since I sent a parcel to Aryana along with a small letter. But I am not sure whether she liked it or not. If you are in contact with her, can you please tell her that I have moved to Canada?' he requested.

'Yes, sure. I will. Should I wait till you get a new number?' she assured him and asked.

'No, Tarang. I won't share my number with anyone just yet. Please, I need some time to heal from my past. Thank you. Thank you for contacting me; I felt light and happy. I hope our paths may cross again when I come back. Bye!'

'Bye Bhargav.' she said.

Tarang narrated the whole conversation to Aryana, and she was shocked.

'What?!' She covered her mouth with both hands. 'I did not receive anything.' She was about to cry.

'Tarang, I have to find it. It must be somewhere in the post office.

But I never gave him my address. Then how did he send it? Are you sure he sent it to me? Or someone else?' She was confused and full of questions.

'Aryana, stop over thinking. Don't lose hope. Calm down. Let's check the post office first,' Tarang said.

They headed to the post office to enquire, but there was no courier. Bhargav, by now, had ported his number to a Canadian number and deleted all social media. It was difficult to contact him. But Aryana and Tarang were confident that the courier was lost. Aryana decided not to give up and hunt the courier down. A week later, she finally tracked it to another post office in a different area. But the addressee's name was hers. "Dr Aryana." It was all because the address was incomplete. She took it home and opened it. There was a letter and a plastic-wrapped box. The letter read,

"Dear Aryana,

I am posting this just a few hours before I leave the country. I have a confession to make, I hope you don't mind. I had a very serious crush on you for a long time. I loved you. I trusted you and respected you. I prayed for you at every point in my life, but I had to convince myself that we have different destinies.

Nevertheless, I just want to say to you, please don't lose hope to live and love, these two things never leave; they bring people together. Close your eyes and promise yourself that you will never think that you have lost hope to live and love. Every time you think like that, I will be in your memories to remind you that hope is still alive. With this letter, I am sending you some hope. Use it well.

Someday, our paths will cross again, because – hope!

With love

Bhargav"

She burst into tears as she opened the wrapper of the parcel. She was filled with regret for not confessing her feelings at the right time. Gathering herself again, she wiped her tears and tried to see if it was still possible to contact him by any means, just to tell him that she loved his gift. But nothing worked as they had no mutual friends except Tarang. Finally, she decided to keep the letter for the rest of her life and accepted the fact that things with him were supposed to end like this. She found peace amidst the chaos.

2036

Abhimanyu was shocked to see a splendid painting of a man holding a lighthouse on his palm, with his eyes sparkling in the sunlight. Astonished Vartika held Abhimanyu's arms and he asked the manager.

'Excuse me, may I know who made this painting? There is no signature.'

A lady standing behind him overheard and said, 'Hello sir. I am Dr Aryana. I have made this painting. How may I help you?'

'Oh! Dr Aryana, this person...' Abhimanyu pointed to the painting.

'He was a childhood friend of mine.' Dr Aryana interrupted.

After a pause, Abhimanyu said, 'The person in the painting is our father, Bhargav Joshi. And I am glad you received those paintbrush sets and oil paint sets in the parcel well.'

Dr Aryana was shocked, and she couldn't believe her ears. Her eyes were tearful as she pulled out a worn-out, decades-old envelope from her pocket and handed it over to Abhimanyu.

'Will you please give this to your father?' she shakily asked, holding his hand.

Abhimanyu nodded.

The letter read,

"*Bhargav, it's been a long time since I felt happy and calm. Thank you for bringing hope into my life again. This is the best gift I have ever received, and I shall treasure it for eternity.*

With hugs,

Aryana"

Part IV

~ Heavy concerns take a rest
When wisdom flows in the quest ~

Illusions

by Jayanti Sabdani

There is no one reason
Of why we do what we do
Perhaps aeons of sensibility
Be quoted perfect for all that is
We create rush and crave for hush
We live thinking of all we are left to live
And when we think, we live the fact of all
And perhaps all of it, we never live.

Aren't we too simple to give each thought a world?
Or too complex, tired to hold ourselves
Our own ears, an abode for opinions
And our own words we bemuse.

We solidify what has always been strong
And our own fantasy we think, is only meant for fancy
Then what we love and love to think, we live with our sweet
phantom
Just wishing to truly wish, that one day it were real

And then, with being said and done like every being does
We step in for what really matters
And each day, come back and wonder –
Why couldn't I do what I should have?
Then we resolve our steps and walk unabated
And it's no wonder we find ourselves saying
After a lot of courage that it was not our call
And in that instance, we wish to pick something from our fancy
lot
And when we do it, we know how it feels
To feel free, to mix things up,
Some reality, some illusion
And despite all, aren't we all happy snails in our own little world?
Of illusions where our mind is the substance,
Where our speed is the hallmark and
Our words, the perfect script.

It's Time to Think and Act Now

by Anju Gupta

Amidst the dead, the wounded, the stranded,
We hear the silent cries for justice.
Of people, who migrated away from their loved ones
Of people, suffering from hunger
Of people, being looted and cheated
Is this the world we dreamt of?
Are we proud to be humans?
It's time to think and think, again.

We hear the silent cries for justice
Of 5-year-olds being raped
Of women being harassed and abused
In their own houses and on the roads
Of the 21-year-olds, who never came back home
And we stand helpless with our vacant and staring eyes.
Is this the world we dreamt of?
It's time to think and think, again.

We hear the silent cries for justice
Of women being stabbed and charred
By their own kith & kin and by the demons roaming free
Of the girl child being killed in the womb
Of the daughter who was married in exchange of a car,
Few kilos of gold and many thousands of rupees
Is this the world we dreamt of?
It's time to think and think, again.

We hear the silent cries for justice
Of thousands gathering to silently protest against the rapists
Of parents who want their daughters to be safe
Of girls who have the right to roam freely even when it's dark
Who should we blame?
The governments, the police, or the judiciary?
Or the common man who silently suffers the inflicted pain?
Or should we just blame ourselves?
For compromising to live this life,
For not standing up for our rights,
For forgetting quite conveniently the last rape, the last murder,
Or the last domestic abuse.
It's time to think and think, again.

Let's respect her, not just as a woman, not just being a girl,
Not just because she is your mother or your wife,
Not just as your sister or your aunt,
Also, not just because she is your daughter,
But because she is a whole generation in herself
And for generations to come.
It's time to act and act, now.

Let's treat her with respect and dignity.
Let's fight with her for peace and justice.
Let's be her ally and support her future openly.
Let's remunerate her the same as him for the same job.
Let's promote her achievements.
Let the stereotypes no longer define her.
Let's nurture a generation of equality.
It's time to act and act. Now.

– An awakened citizen

Legacy

by Kruttika R. Hegde

What do you leave behind for us?
Broken morals and superstitions
A mountain of rules to follow
An image to guard with our lives
Why does it all seem so hollow?
Why this burden on the shoulders?
Of a generation, who live by their dreams
What do you leave behind for us?
Your legacy that we must keep alive
Look within, is all really well?
Can you look at your reflection and say,
You have done right by you?
Can you really say the life you lived,
The lessons you learned,
The ethics you lived by were ideal?
What do you leave behind for us?
A tainted legacy and a boost to your ego?

We would like to move beyond

Live by our dreams

We cannot carry the torch of your legacy,

We leave it behind

We cannot carry the torch of your legacy,

The flame will burn our souls

In the darkest night

We will not carry your legacy and hand it those who come after

We will look beyond

That legacy tainted with blood and sorrow and oppression of the
weak

Your legacy will burn tonight.

The Ambivalence of Hope

by C.L.Y.

To many, amidst hateful screams or deafening silence,
Hope is the lullaby that calms and soothes.
That small but undying flicker of light from within
That fights on relentlessly in the name of truth.
Hope is alive outside a critical operation room
And within the walls of places of worship.
It thrives in the hearts of risk-taking entrepreneurs,
And it is abundant before, during, and after an exam for the
youth.

Hope fuels the dreams that idealists pursue,
Hope is the backbone of all creations new.

But what is hope to an ailing, suffering patient,
Or to a child stuck in an unhealthy home?
What is hope to the societal minorities
Whose struggles are marginalised and still unknown?
Is hope a faithful, encouraging promise
Of a future that will be better than today?

Or is hope the sweetest but fruitless lie
That never delivers and has a heart of stone?

Hope is an emotion many have learnt not to show –
It only disappoints and breaks them, blow after blow.

Arbitrary successes make us or break us,
In this universe so absurd and life so chaotic and wild.
Hope is wanting that chance to favour our wishes,
Hope is wishing humans looked at each other with love and
smiled.
Hope can lift us up or utterly crush us to tears,
And yet we dare to persevere and hope again.
Humanity is perhaps the most beautiful tragedy,
And hope is humans showing their dauntless inner child.

Hope is staying alive through and facing every trial,
Hope is a reason to make our short, worthless yet priceless lives
worthwhile.

The Real Me

by Krishna

Break looks like time lost
Smile wears a fake gloss
Canned child waiting inside to pound
Yet the fear to show the real me
Has made myself lose me
Why does it always exist?
Why does the cost of my happiness
Hide behind the opinions of the rest?
Melody of the dove alone
Is what seeming to me the best
Alluring me high as a cat's nappiness
What weighs in the snappiness?
Calm down, slow down
Hush off and heads down
No more madness around
Is this why everyone's around?
To meet and then curb the sound
What discipline fades in expressing faith?

Trust me nothing is wrong if you are straight
Love to either stay away or hang out
The choice rests on me
Because I am not bound but free.
Roots of all my queries lie
In the process to eliminate every block
Will dance in the rain, save some gain
Lick the mist and skip the gist
Because my key to being content
Is just simply not to repent
Have learnt to scrap the meek inside
And add mirth nutrition to life
Because my happiness lies in the real me
And that is where I will always be.

Vanquishing Insecurities

by Arijit Dey

Dealing with insecurities that the society doesn't talk about and address, we grow up in a post-modern era where the word 'insecurities' has been stereotyped with women. But we often tend to forget the other side of the coin; a gender that exists and is loved only when it provides any value, still supporting in daily lives' patriarchal struggles of their counterparts, waking up every day to be judged by looks, thoughts, and profession, with a smile at each and every moment.

You can't complain, you can't cry,
From childhood to manhood, you still try.
You are taught to be strong,
Feeble-minded are always judged as wrong.
For there are others,
Who may have talked on your back once,
Hurting your sole existence all at once.

But I suggest....

Let us break the shackles of this prison of yours,
Which you have caged within yours.
Speak out every moment, express out every emotion,
The world is lacking those real-life "emoticons",
Which may bind individuals together,
Which you have always kept as a placeholder.
Judging will always be there, it's up to you to fight and face;
Create your own vibe, making it a better phase,
Enjoy your own company, enhancing your place.
Till the time you come across people who value your thoughts;
Let your heart speak out, the things that hover in your mind,
That will make this race remind,
Of someone out there, who is fighting his own fight,
Letting out his thoughts which may not have been in sight.

Insecurities lie everywhere,
From relationships to bank balance,
You have hundreds of reasons to worry,
But let the world know you have a hundred more to smile about.
As the saying goes, "Dance first, think later!"
Take decisions first, make them worth it later.
Set back only when you have second thoughts,
Not when someone criticizes yours.

The world is out there waiting for you to be free,

Free from the bondages and insecurities which you have curled up within.

For there lie flaws everywhere,

It is sometimes good to be perfectly imperfect

Even a flawed diamond is still a diamond.

Be that hero, messiah to your story,

Give your thoughts a chance to stand the world;

Else it will just fade away like a dream,

No matter how much you later scream.

For those who ever questioned your feelings and thoughts,

Let them know when you come back strong.

This world needs people to be more transparent,

Transparent in value and thoughts.

Not bogged down by some historical judging element,

Come let us create this life a better place, free from stereotypes and judgment.

The Myth and the Fact

by Archana Sanjay Avhad

The year 2022 is already here. None of us would have ever thought that the whole world would suffer from such a painful and daunting experience of Covid-19. From being declared as a public health emergency to becoming a global pandemic within the blink of an eye, the world was introduced to a series of 'lockdowns' which eventually became the new normal.

Today when I look back at those days, my heart aches painfully after watching people breathing for the last time, becoming unemployed and homeless and my hands feel tied with the rope of my own problems, that even if I sincerely want to help, I won't be able to make much of a difference.

Heartbeats escalating
Minds freezing
World order disrupted
Havoc all around.
Nights getting darker
Sunshine losing its warmth
Evenings full of dilemma
Can't decide what is right

Is there life in problems?
Or are there problems in life?
Wishes so many to fulfil
But now, only a few left to survive
Countable people and tears infinite
Passing time brings more conditions in life.
Nothing stays forever
This time will also end
Shivering hands will stay strong
And we'll achieve that peace of mind
Our hearts will again glow.
At last!
When everything will get alright
Imagining that scenario my soul feels light
No more sorrows and fingers crossed
The world will be ours and we will stand together
Through the highs and the lows.
Only if I could explain in few words,
I would want a world with less of misery
And with a little more of life.

It was 11:15 on just another Wednesday night, I was scrolling through posts on my phone and there suddenly popped up a random article saying that when people die, they have 7 minutes of brain activity left, in which they are able to play back memories in a dream sequence. I don't even know if it is true or not, but many people call it a myth and many consider it a fact; after all, everyone has their own belief system which is never entirely identical for all.

The next day, my mother asked me to accompany her to visit the Sai Temple (Sai Baba Mandir) in our town. It is nearly 4000 steps away from our residence by walking distance.

We started early in the morning around 7:30 a.m. and reached there within 25 to 30 minutes. Early morning walks are a pure bliss and what made our walk more special was the fact that it was the first time after Covid-19 that I had stepped out of my house, and it was like a cherry on cake for me.

On my way, I had a close look on all the activities that were happening. There was a man who was selling masks, dogs were wandering and barking, the shopkeepers were looking after their products and the road was busy with vehicles as usual, some moving in the similar direction like a queue of ants, but the hush and rush was not like the way it used to be earlier, mainly due to the pandemic.

While returning home, we took a bus as both of us were tired and it literally felt like it had been ages since we had a good walk, and it indeed had been. I was sitting near the window watching the view outside. Nothing had changed in the half hour since I observed it on our way to the temple.

That one man was still selling masks; the dogs were still wandering and barking, the shopkeepers were still doing their business and the road was still busy. The place, the situation and the person observing it all was the same, and the only difference was the time. Earlier, it took 30 minutes while now it took only 5.

The pleasure of sitting on a window seat was so refreshing, and then, the thought popped up in my mind that how radical our lives could be. A random thing I heard last night affected me on such a level that my observation and perspective took a different course. It taught me the value of this life and the time we are left with. I thought and thought and kept on thinking. I am still confused about whether it's a myth or a fact but now, I have decided to live every moment of my life to its best, that the day when my whole life flashes before my eyes, it's worth watching with no place for regrets. My soul will happily welcome all those memories with me being proud of myself for the times I didn't give up even when life broke me into thousands of pieces. Now, I am afraid of wasting even a single second of my life. All I want is to celebrate every little thing that this life graces me with.

When times were hard
And people were harder,
When surroundings were dark
And truth was darker,
I got up and fought those battles
Like a warrior fighting on the battlefield.

All that matters today is 'today' and I'll try my level best to make today the best day of my life.

Vibrant Lights

by C.L.Y.

The light bulbs turned off.

All around me, a blanket of still silence fell over,

As one by one, a hundred lights flickered into existence.

Ambient music gave me company in an otherwise empty room,

As the world at large around me battled on against a pandemic.

I just stood there against the window,

A million thoughts ablaze in my head,

And a million emotions,

The most prominent one being awe.

Awe at the sight of so many different people coming together to
help against a common threat

By appreciating those doing the real work –

Fighting the disease and healing the victims.

More than that,

Awe at the wave of positivity spreading out from this act,

Something much needed in these dark times.

Earlier, it was clapping,
The collective sound of which still echoes in my ears till today,
And now, lighting up the dark –
Hope.

This is evidence that the world can come together despite
differences, if need be,
Because who are we if we don't stand united in times like this?
What is humanity if it doesn't stand as one despite individual
differences?
Empathy and unity in diversity make us human.
The light-show around me still blazed on,
And my spirit was also ablaze with the beauty of it all.

The glass of my window became foggy as I leaned onto it,
And all I could see were a blur of multicoloured lights,
Twinkling and pulsating and emitting vibrant auras,
In every direction visible,
Just like stars.

And just like the stars glittering across the night sky,
The sight was heavenly, alluring, bewitching.
I looked up to see the stars twinkling above
And with all my heart, whispered a plea –
"Help us through this."

And through the sight I beheld around me,
The universe whispered back,
Reminding me that nothing in creation is permanent,
Energising me as the power of hope flowed through me,
With words so comforting and warm and tender and nothing
short of truth –
"This, too, shall pass."

What If?

by Vanshika Gupta

We mostly live so uptight
Wishing for things so upright
Losing the mere chance to work it
Making way for a better stride
An ocean of emotions guiding the lane
With all the efforts going in vain
Hoping to have the best shot
The rising disgust says it all.

What if the vacant spaces are filled again?
Carrying a toll of emotions in the headspace
A handful of regrets
A heart full of contempt
Loading the air with fresh sight of intent
A mind full of moments and memories
Taking away your only treasury
You believe you can do it
One more attempt to delay the destination.

But what if all that you needed?
Was knocking on your doorstep
Little more courage assured
You could be victorious
By waving goodbye to all the drifters
You could accept a happy failure
By leaving behind all the traitors
That you had been growing inside out.

Just a footstep of distance
A little less of confusion
A little more of faith
What if all that you needed?
Was just a small sign
Of truly living through your blessings
Regardless of how perfectly
To just get going ahead
Happily, and heartily!

What is the Goal of our Life?

by Vishal Nagpal

What is the goal of our life?
While cutting the cake with a beautiful knife.
Did we ever introspect, what's the goal of our life?

I tried asking people, what's the goal of their life?
'A Big House', 'An Empire', 'A Rich Husband' or 'A Beautiful
Wife'.
The answers I got were only increasing my rife!
I'm not convinced! Could someone tell me the profound goal of
our life?

It's not about big or small, good, or bad – it is a different strife.
What is the profound goal of life?
They said, think twice!
I rather tried thrice –
O Life! I don't know, I'm not that wise!

Let me tell you clear and concise:

Hell, or heaven – it's all here! There's no farther paradise.

You got to live here! Stop looking for a distant paradise.

Quest is to know the core of life; it won't be as easy as you throw a dice.

Admirable is always the one who tries,

Not the one that cries.

Let us all try and find the answer: What is the purpose of this life?

And while struggling to resolve this strife

Let us not forget to play the drum and the melodious fife!

O, my joyful Life!

You're a beautiful journey, I must rejoice!

There's no destination, why are worries so rife?

Each day is a wonderful station, unfurling 'the banner of joy' is my choice!

We're born to be joyfully alive!

My dear friend, don't just survive.

Live each day, revive!

Life is an ocean of love, why don't you make a dive?

Why?

by Rinku Tyagi

Why has the sun lost its colour?
Why are the flowers bereft of smell?
Why everything around me seems,
So tasteless and dull; just can't tell.

Just yesterday, everything was fine,
What changed today, listless I feel,
Life has come to a standstill,
It's something I'm not ready to deal with.

Foggy consciousness of my brain,
Wants to shut itself down,
Not ready to accept; not able to bear,
In the passiveness, my heart may drown.

Lovely thoughts like never born,
Carefree mind has far long gone,
Once light in my steps; no more,
Cheerful, sunny countenance bygone.

Sometimes from behind the gloomy clouds,
A bright ray of hope peeks,
Shadowed by the hideous thoughts,
Goes scurrying in the deepest creeks.

May the light touch me again,
And I feel the caress of the cool breeze,
May I feel a bounce in my heart,
Wounds may heal, pain may freeze.

Wide Awake, I Feel Great!

by Vishal Nagpal

Wide awake, I feel great!
I won't rush for the race straight,
Let us be a little mindful, wait!
I'm in no hurry, are you getting late?
Let us be a little aware, a brand-new day awaits.

On this new day, who will decide my fate?
If I am the creator, what should I create?
If I can actually create,
How would I do it, what is that secret?
'Faith', 'hard work', 'courage', among the words that I relate.
If we can actually create,
Let's create it together with all the love and no hate!

I'm told to earn,

But what is to be earnt?

Learning a few lessons,

A lot many to be learnt!

For a mindful experience of life,

I'm so thankful!

What's the point of having a wealthy life?

If by the end of the day you're not grateful.

If we can actually create,

Let's create it together with all the love

and no hate!

I reinstate,

all the love, no hate!

Zest's Wake-Up Call

by Vanshika Gupta

How often do we peep into our past lives but forget to keep track
of the time?

How often do we react to all the negatives but don't pay heed to
the negativity inside us?

How often do we follow the footsteps, but cease to go out of our
comfort zones?

How often do we judge for intentions, but are always in denial of
our own intuition?

How often do we allow our confidence to drop, but never drop
our rigid thinking?

How often do we demand love but forget to love our own selves
first?

How often do we search for humanity but don't recognise
goodness?

For we think we have time,

But the truth is that we all like to live in illusions.

For we think we can get over it,

But the truth is that we are drawn towards it even more.

For we think everyone is eventually going to hurt us,

But the truth is that we hurt ourselves more.

For we think reality is hard to accept,

But the truth is that the idea of coming out of our fantasies is
harder.

For we think this world can be made a better place to live in,

But the truth is that we live inside our imagination.

For we think living is gruelling,

But the truth is that we don't make efforts to live a little better.

Thus,

When harmony within the self comes to a halt

I hope you find the courage to host

The perfect life you wished for

It won't be easy for sure

As the world would seem to distort

But hang in there, dear human!

For you still have so much to live for

You will get through this

As soon as you find the harmonising power

Within and in the world

You are a part of.

Acknowledgements

I thank the entire team of Inkfeathers Publishing from the core of my heart for giving me the opportunity to create this anthology and for extending their support, trust, and guidance throughout this process. Working with such an affable and quality organisation, I have learnt a lot and all of it has been a great stimulus to my growth, both personally and professionally.

This project wouldn't have been possible without the beautiful and wholesome contribution made by my co-authors, and I thank each and every one of them for believing in me and in this anthology and for bringing our 'A Little More of Life' to life.

I'm grateful to my family and friends for making me believe that I could do justice to this project and for always being my pillars of strength. I want to express my deepest gratitude to my father. His frequent use of idioms in our daily conversations instilled a deep love for words in me.

Last but not the least, a huge shoutout to 'A Little More of Life' that didn't let me lose my hope in its successful completion and reminded me why it was being created in the first place, to instil the idea of living a little more, with imperishable faith and hope.

Meet the
Co-Authors

Arijit Dey *(@arijitzzzzz)*

Arijit Dey is a Mechanical Engineering graduate from BITS Pilani with his prime interest in the domain of supply chain and finance. Apart from his professional engagement in a full-time job in an MNC, he is passionate about exploring new things and technologies. A budding writer who loves reading medieval & colonial history, mentoring competitive-exam aspirants and a big sports enthusiast.

Rinku Tyagi *(@tyagii_rrinnku)*

Rinku Tyagi is an educator; poet; writer and the author of an anthology of poems 'Memoirs of a Wedded Mind' available on Amazon. Besides writing poems, Rinku also writes blogs for her website www.poetic-resonance.com. She truly believes that an ignited mind can change the world.

Kruttika R. Hegde *(Twitter @Moon_Struck78)*

Lively, fun loving and a passionate reader, Kruttika has spent her life delving into the unending beauty of literature and poetry. She believes that words are magical in the way they can bring to life the imaginative worlds trapped in layers of a mind.

Ashon Calhoun *(@cal_the_creator)*

Ashon Calhoun is 22 years old and has been writing since he was 6. He had his first poem published at 8. Poetry has become a major part of him over the years and its involvement in his life is increasing. He loves poetry and he hopes you will love his work, too.

Nuzhat Reza *(@namelessriot)*

A Dhaka born-and-bred, proud Bengali but also a Londoner at heart and home, Nuzhat's passion follows a pen that stems from the breadth of her own experience and sentiments cultivated through time, relationships, cultures, languages and mostly life as it happened. She has a degree and a master's in finance and works in the corporate world, but she writes to connect to people, to bond on mutual sentiments and to encourage one another with words of wisdom and truth.

Zoya Hussain *(@zoe._.25)*

She is Zoya, eponymous with the Greek 'Zoe', meaning 'life'. In a nutshell, she is just her name – zealous, vibrant and lively. Out of the various forms of expressions that a human uses, writing strikes her the most. Her compositions are mostly a reflection of life; partly sweet, partly sour.

Yesha Dave (*@yesha__dave*)

An engineer with a knack for writing, Yesha seeks the power to realise the abstract in life. With a mind full of thoughts and a heart full of emotions, writing is a means of catharsis to her. A stickler for discipline, and a sucker for short stories, she lives a reclusive life, brave enough to not conform to the "ideal" life.

Aditi Rao

Aditi Rao is somebody who is trying to find more to the life we all live. A believer in the existence of misfits who fit into an alternate reality, Aditi earns, pens and revels in life experiences of people around her. Have an experience? Feel free to connect with her rao.aditi06@gmail.com.

Apurav Mahajan

An engineer by profession, writer by passion and an ardent sketcher, Apurav Mahajan comes from the UT of Jammu & Kashmir. Brought up in Delhi and Chandigarh, he is a people's person, who loves writing quotes and poems about life, romance and everything which makes you think deep within. You can read more of his writings by searching for "Apurav Mahajan Quotes". No, seriously, try it! :)

Simran Gupta

Simran is indeed a very polite and decent girl. Her talent of expressing views in the form of poetry is amazing. Creative, fun-loving, music lover, and charming is what she is made of.

Matali Mahajan

Matali is an ambivert and is now working as a research scholar in Economics. She is a lover and admirer of old Bollywood songs. Reading poems and quotes gives her the motivation to move forward and break her boundaries.

Tashu Malik (*@the_eternal_ephemeral*)

Tashu is an active social worker who runs an educational centre for underprivileged children while also being associated with other NGOs. True to her Piscean nature, she describes herself as a die-hard dreamer and even a utopian. Her writing speaks of the ephemeral nature of life which keeps trying to find its place within the eternal truths of existence.

Pratheepa Kannan

Pratheepa is a banker-turned-content-writer, pursuing her passion towards becoming a published author. She is inquisitive about worldly emotions and loves to put into words. Poetry writing is her solace in the tough days. She aspires to leave an imprint of her writings in this world. She believes words are the best way to express a human mind. She is on the path to become an author and a content strategist.

Dani Hudson (*@angel_archives_*)

Dani is a self-proclaimed novice poet and prose writer from Missouri. She sees writing as a means of connection; a way to make the intangible tangible.

Raghav Mahajan (*@raghav.rocco*)

Raghav has completed his BBA and engineering; he is just a normal guy who doesn't know where he belongs, and so, trying his luck out in the hope that this is the one he truly desires.

Raghav Sharma

Raghav Sharma, also known by his pen name #Ra, is a finance lad, crazy about anything, but more for hiking in novels and mountains.

Rohan P. Lapalikar (*@author.rohanpel*)

Rohan hails from Mumbai. He is a teacher by profession, also a comic, and a passionate photographer by hobby. He loves writing fictional stories and poems. He believes that "This world is made up of not just atoms and molecules, but also stories." He is a compassionate animal lover as well.

Vishal Nagpal (*@uttertheflutter*)

Vishal Nagpal is a working professional. Through his poetry, he is trying to utter the flutter of his heart. For him, poetry is a great medium of expression of thoughts and emotions. His poetry works include odes around paternal love and gratitude, philosophy of life and human inquisitiveness.

Namrata Agarwal (@_namrata_15)

Namrata Agarwal is the founder of Vishisht Lifestyle, an eco-friendly brand offering natural skincare products made using clean and pure ingredients and delivered in low-waste packaging. She enjoys travelling, watching sitcoms, journalling, listening to podcasts, reading books and articles on self-development, mental health, etc. She is an animal lover.

Malvika Sharma

Malvika is a budding ophthalmologist, maintaining her passion to pen down visionary thoughts.

Shabnam Islam (@phantasm_of_past)

New she is in a world of unknowns, trying to write something worth which can change the words untold. Shabnam is a writer by fate, storyteller for the world, poetess is what she wants to be; Co-author of many publication houses including Inkfeathers Publishing, Young minds publication, Wordsgenix and many more to come because it's a never-ending journey for her as a writer.

Mansha Kapoor *(@xmanshax)*

Meet the Wizard of Words, Mansha. She is best friends with Alice of the wonderland, they often discuss the theories of Sherlock Holmes over tea. You will find her in the snow-capped mountains, riding about on her bike, capturing beautiful moments by day, and creating spell-binding stories by night.

Mohammed Sadiq *(@_poet_j_)*

Mohammed Jafer Sadiq, an engineer by profession, always found it difficult to communicate and express himself to others. To overcome this, he started writing his feelings down about people and the things around. This helped him discover his passion for writing, earlier which he failed to appreciate.

Shay P. Kris *(@iceprincess_2296)*

Digital marketer, chef and now poet and author! It seems there is nothing Shay can't do. She usually writes when inspiration strikes her and when it doesn't, she is researching what next to write on. In her spare time, she curls up on her sofa watching 90's sitcoms and watching over the cooking.

Ashyl Elizabath Paul

Ashyl is a Bengaluru-based journalist, writer, a great listener, and believes in a better world.

Angela Sharon

Angela has been a passionate writer but without a place to express herself, now breaking all chains and rising to make difference is her purpose. She's also striving to be a psychologist to help people and bring a smile to their faces.

A. Prakruthi (*@deepthi_praku*)

A. Prakruthi is a Law graduate and a poet who writes to express her heart out. Her strength is her dad who is also an advocate and her boon companion.

Rakhee Daryanani *(@socialswithrakhs)*

Rakhee is an aviation enthusiast and now working as a freelancer in content writing and social media management. She is an ardent lover of travel and collecting boarding passes is her hobby. She is a devotee of Bollywood music and singing is her passion.

Varun Ahuja *(@varunnn_ahuja)*

Varun is a fiction story creator, trying his hands in various fields and will usually be found goofing around at Riverfront, Ahmedabad. With a bundle of ideas to implement, he has made multiple accomplishments. Often procrastinated in pitching his thoughts, he is now finally bringing his stories on paper.

Neeraja Krishnaswami *(@nkaysfictionalparadise)*

Neeraja Krishnaswami is a Postgraduate in Business Management, an Accounts Executive with her father and a blogger by choice. Writing being her passion, she has participated in poetry and story writing competitions and is a co-author in anthologies. Apart from writing, her hobbies are singing, painting and landscape photography.

Puja Bordoloi

"Life opens up to you in numerous chapters, to live, learn and grow." This 22-year-old girl from Assam is an optimist in search of the perfect definition of life. Besides being a writer, Puja is also a motivational speaker, currently working for mental health upliftment of the society. She believes in the reflection of happiness when one feels the same. Currently, she is pursuing a master's degree in chemistry.

C.L.Y.

C.L.Y. is a young artist who loves creating and expressing art in many forms. Going by the motto "I was created to create; I exist to question existence," C.L.Y. is an existentialist who loves philosophy, psychology, and literature, with a keen desire to learn and an aspiration to help humanity.

Chetan Singh Manhas

Chetan is a man with an ambition to explore the world and live his life to the fullest.

Krishna

Krishna is a graduate in BA Political Science Honours and is a resident of Punjab. She adopted the medium of writing to promote the drive of self-care. Her poem 'The Real Me' is an attempt to normalise embracing one's real self, peel the layers of imitation off for sake of selection and have a little more of life.

Anju Gupta *(@gupta.anju9)*

Anju Gupta is a seasoned Education Management industry leader who has authored research papers on educational topics. Her services in the field of education have been recognized by educational organisations felicitating her with awards in various categories. Her views on education and other related topics are regularly published in print and digital media. Her poetic pieces are based on the hard facts and challenging experiences of life which hit deep into the hearts of listeners/readers. Her writing and narration acumen has been recognised at various platforms and appreciated by one and all. She is active on major social media platforms.

Archana Sanjay Avhad *(@elysianxasa)*

Archana is a 20-year-old girl pursuing her studies in the Management field and loves to empower her thoughts through her words. She likes to read books, visit new places, meet new people, and discover new little happiness in her everyday life.

Jayanti Sabdani *(@beyond.being_)*

Jayanti is a content writer and a poet. She takes the philosophical fibre in her writings to express what is inexpressible, abstract, and seemingly insignificant.

INKFEATHERS PUBLISHING

India's Most Author Friendly Publishing House

Stay updated about the latest books, anthologies, events, exclusive offers, contests, product giveaways and other things that we do to support authors.

 Inkfeathers Publishing

 @InkfeathersPublishing

 @_Inkfeathers

 @Inkfeathers

 Inkfeathers.com

We'd love to connect with you!

9 789390 882151